*Night in
Erg Chebbi
and Other
Stories*

The

Iowa

Short

Fiction

Award

In honor of

James O. Freedman

University of

Iowa Press

Iowa City

*Edward
Hamlin*

*Night in
Erg Chebbi
and Other
Stories*

University of Iowa Press, Iowa City

University of Iowa Press, Iowa City 52242

Copyright © 2015 by Edward Hamlin

www.uiowapress.org

Printed in the United States of America

No part of this book may be reproduced or used in any form
or by any means without permission in writing from the
publisher. All reasonable steps have been taken to contact
copyright holders of material used in this book. The
publisher would be pleased to make suitable arrangements
with any whom it has not been possible to reach. This is a
work of fiction; any resemblance to actual events or persons
is entirely coincidental.

The University of Iowa Press is a member of Green Press
Initiative and is committed to preserving natural resources.
Printed on acid-free paper

Library of Congress Cataloging-in-Publication Data
Hamlin, Edward.
Night in Erg Chebbi and other stories / Edward Hamlin.
pages   cm
ISBN 978-1-60938-383-1 (pbk)
ISBN 978-1-60938-384-8 (ebk)
I. Title.
PS3608.A69545A6 2015
813'.6—dc23   2015005545

Contents

ACKNOWLEDGMENTS

It's with true pleasure that I'd like to thank these close readers and close friends for helping bring this book to life: Paula and Mary Hamlin, Karen Yost, Eve Sneed, Julie Goldstein, the Tuesday Night Writers, Antoinette Mehler and Charles Paddack, Margaret Strumpf, Karen and Steve Frankel, J. Tamar Stone, Steve Reinthal, David Blatt and David Moore. Thanks also to Lisa Roberts for her insights on Morocco; to Sean Montgomery for certain Northern Irish correctives; to Alexander Hamlin for teaching me the grammar of canine behavior; to Ling Ling Church for the chilling after-dinner tale that inspired "One Child Policy"; and to the Colorado firefighters who kept hammering at the 2010 Fourmile Canyon Fire though they knew their own homes might be in harm's way. These stories are stronger for your generosity and inspiration.

Lastly, my sincere thanks to the editors, contest judges, and other literary friends who've brought my work to the page and the stage: Jim Shepard, Karen Russell, Danielle Ofri, Stacy Bodziak, Anthony Powell, Stephanie G'Schwind, Steven Schwartz, Katherine Hill, E. J. Levy, Elizabeth Taylor, Jennifer Day, Speer Morgan, Evelyn Somers, Michael Nye, James Esch, Tom Jenks, Eli Weiss, Triska Tropova, and not least the University of Iowa Press team.

This book is dedicated to my mother, Mary Hamlin, and my wife, Paula Hamlin, for holding the tightrope steady while the equilibrist does his thing.

Several of the stories in this collection have previously appeared in literary magazines or been recognized in national competitions.

"Indígena" was a finalist for the 2014 *Missouri Review* Jeffrey E. Smith Editors' Prize and also for *Narrative Magazine*'s Fall 2014 Story Contest. It was published in the Spring 2015 issue of the *Missouri Review*.

"Night in Erg Chebbi" was the 2013 winner of the Nelligan Prize for Fiction, final judge Jim Shepard. It was published in volume 40 of the *Colorado Review*.

Night in
Erg Chebbi
and Other
Stories

Indígena

It wasn't the guns that bothered her but rather the heat, which was the true killing machine. Guns had always been with her; they figured in her earliest memories. Her father dismantling a revolver on the kitchen table as she picked at her greasy Ulster fry. The RUC boys armed to the teeth outside the greengrocer's smashed door, outfitted for war in a dank city street. High-powered rifles with sniper scopes laid out in the boot like firewood, or cradled like infants as her uncles stalked through the muddy darkness along the right-of-way. Guns were cityscape. By the age of twelve she could identify make and model from a ten-yard remove and judge ammunition by the results it fetched: peering down from the second floor of the grammar school as boys shot pigeons off ledges, she could guess the caliber by the damage done. When she turned fourteen, her brother Roddy made sure she had her own pistol, a battered Webley, and knew when to use it.

Despite himself, Moore had been impressed with her expertise when they met. It was in the first days after the flood, when men were still sandbagging the riverbank and women tracked red mud from house to house, the rainforest floor roiling with steam. The humidity was absolute.

"Classic Widowmaker there," she'd said from the adjacent table, a grilled *tamuatá* untouched before her. An AR-18 was slung over the guest chair opposite him. It was not uncommon for local men to carry hunting rifles, whether to shoot marauding strays or take boar, but an automatic weapon in the possession of a gringo was another matter. "Japanese or American?"

Moore regarded her without emotion, as was his way even with close associates and lovers, his pitted face a perfect mask. He waited for her as if he'd been the one to pose the question. But men no longer intimidated her, and she stared at him with clean concentration, refusing to back down. After a methodical sip of beer he said: "American. '72."

"Brilliant. Gas ring holding up?"

She saw a calculation ripple across Moore's forehead, where you could sometimes read his thoughts. She'd got his attention. Possibly he'd never met a woman who could talk weaponry with such composure and mastery. "Thing is," she said, "over time that ring'll fail you and you'll short-stroke. You won't get one bloody round off." She saw him straighten in his cane chair, shift his stocky shoulders awkwardly. He would prefer it if she left, per-haps—or failing that, stepped over to dine with him. "I'm Maeve, by the way. And your own good self?"

By way of reply he turned his chair half away from her, which at the same time left it half facing her.

She knew the evening mosquitoes would soon roam in from the river, moving across the open-air patio in ragged death squads. Tontons Macoutes, she called them, but the joke was lost on every-one. The locals knew almost nothing of Manaus, much less of Haiti. What still shocked her was that the American eco-tourists didn't follow her, either—her guests might have the wherewithal to travel from Chicago or Kansas City to the Brazilian interior, but they had no more knowledge of history than a back-country *indígeno*. They knew nothing of the Troubles, nothing of the Duvalier bloodbath—nothing of her world. Disgraceful, but their ignorance protected her.

She could see the lolling river from where she sat, the water brown as shoe leather, foul-smelling and noxious since the rains had washed the shantytown away. The makeshift hovels had been well upstream, far out of town, but day by day one saw more evidence of them as the river continued to lick at the remains. Corpses had been spotted drifting past, the odd sling chair or Styrofoam cooler, bloated dogs and feral pigs, a buoyant crucifix swirling in an eddy as if possessed by the soul of a dervish. Mangrove roots trapped petrol cans, hats, bottles. The carnage had quickly driven the late-season tourists away, starting with the Kapsteins, young New Yorkers who'd been staying in Treetop Lodge 1 with its perfect view of the fetid watercourse. Maeve refunded their money without argument. Two Canadian couples were expected at the weekend; she wondered if they'd heard.

Without tourists the town deflated, its tiny vein of commerce collapsing. She and Moore were the only guests Casa Ribeiro had served in days. She smelled *pinga* on the proprietor's breath tonight, and who could blame him? The drenching heat, the fleeing foreigners, the loss of a cousin in the wash-out—it had hit him hard. Relieved of her normal chores, all five treehouse cabanas empty, she'd been eating lunch and dinner at Casa Ribeiro mostly to make sure Paulo Ribeiro didn't do anything rash. Just now he was drifting toward her table with a worried look, frowning at her fish.

"*O peixe não tá bom, Senhora Kelly?*"

"No," she smiled, "the fish is brilliant. Just in no rush here." He'd insisted it was caught and iced before the flood poisoned the river, an antediluvian fish. To reassure him she took up knife and fork and surgically removed the head, setting it aside for a stray. This seemed satisfactory, and he moved on to his other guest with a swaying step.

When Paulo wandered back to the kitchen she expected the sporadic conversation with Moore to continue in some way, but it did not. He made no eye contact, only finishing his beer and quickly dispatching his grilled chicken. When he was done he laid a large bill on the table, took up the Widowmaker, donned his tarp hat and walked out, his white shirt soaked through in the shape of a giant hand. Only when she heard two car doors slam and saw a Land Rover with darkened windows pull away did Maeve realize that someone had been keeping watch over Moore the whole time, and not only over Moore.

———————

She knew who he was, of course; everyone did. He was the gringo who lived in the razor wire compound perched on a red dirt promontory three miles up the private road, the longest paved stretch in the area. The sprawling house had been built for a would-be cattle rancher who'd died before a single tree could be felled for pastureland. Three years ago, Moore had appeared out of nowhere, bought the place for back taxes and turned it into a fortress, importing workers from a distant charcoal camp disbanded not long before. It was assumed the old man didn't want locals involved for security reasons—an absurd notion, paranoia imported from another world. Speculation was that he was a Colombian involved at the highest levels of the drug trade, perhaps a cartel banker, but she suspected he was just a rich American eccentric, some software millionaire or stock trader living out a colonial fantasy. In the few words they'd exchanged she hadn't noticed a particular accent, but that didn't mean anything in an expat; his name was English, but that meant even less, as one assumed it wasn't his real one.

The man called Moore was self-sufficient and generally invisible, which made her wonder what he was doing here at Paulo's, tucking into a plate of chicken like anyone else. The compound had its own weedy airstrip, a holdover from earlier days; Moore received weekly cargo flights said to deliver not just staples but also French wines and city whores, though this last smelled of hopeful fantasy on the part of the local men. Nor did the gringo rely on anyone else for electricity, fresh water, medical treatment, security. He had generators, purifiers, a staff doctor, a private militia with evident firepower. And he had uplinks: a bristling array of dishes and antennas connected the place with the greater world, including, some thought, a private satellite stationed directly overhead. Because he revealed nothing of himself, all wonders seemed possible.

Maeve's second encounter with Moore, if indirect, came the very morning after meeting him at Casa Ribeiro. As she was fretting over accounts, the Land Rover of the night before deposited two of Moore's palace guards at the gate. Her stomach turned at the sight of them: as a girl of twelve she'd seen just such a Land Rover disgorge two RUC men who'd then put a rifle butt through her cousin's skull alongside the Falls Road. She didn't want this lot on her land. She strode quickly to the gate but didn't unlock it, waiting for them to state their business.

The driver was *mestiço* but the other was pure blue-black, a stunning man in a military-looking uniform. Looking past the pressed khaki, she guessed he'd come up in some Rio or São Paulo slum, as much an outsider here as she was. "Miss Kelly," he said.

"Herself."

"I am Xoque," he said, revealing crude teeth. He pronounced it as in English, *Shock*—just the sort of blustering gang name they gave themselves in the Rio favelas. "Security chief for Mr. Moore." It appeared the brief exchange over Moore's Widow-maker had raised questions.

"What of it?"

Xoque eyed the locked gate; considered his options. He had not expected this reception. At last he said, "Mr. Moore invites you to lunch at your earliest convenience."

"I'm quite busy."

Xoque looked past her, saw the empty treehouses thrown open for airing. "As you like. Perhaps you'll call when you have an opening, Miss Kelly." With exaggerated courtesy he handed a business card through the gate and they were gone, the driver putting boot to the board up the mud-stained road.

Maeve had lived in her skin long enough to recognize an interesting disturbance in the membrane that linked her to the world, a flex of the integument, and she felt it now. Throughout the long day she considered Moore's invitation, and that evening she rang the number on Xoque's card.

———————

The rest of the rainy season passed without the second flood that everyone had so feared. Television warned that such events would be commonplace now, but the swollen months crawled by without incident, with ordinary rain, and slowly the foreigners returned. Maeve was fully booked. She trained a manager to cover for her on the nights she was away at Moore's; the place quickly found its rhythm, her coffers filling steadily. Seven months of clement weather set the stunned village back on its feet. But then the rains arrived a month too soon, not cooling the forest as usual but bringing an onslaught of crippling heat. The turn of events was strange enough to be carried on the national news—a death blow. Her late-season bookings were mostly middle-class Brazilian families on holiday, well able to sacrifice the small deposit, and the final month was gutted. In scarcely a week the cabanas were empty.

Maeve was not at peace with the unseasonable heat. It fulminated, like a kind of racehorse lather you couldn't shake off, the sworn enemy of sleep. Even Haiti had rarely been as bad. By municipal edict the electricity was killed an hour after nightfall, whereupon the electric fans spun down and the ponderous cowl descended. This against a childhood in grey Belfast with its damp and penetrating winter chill.

She slept fitfully, dreaming of broken glass and sirens and whip-like gunshots, fever dreams imposed by the heat and her condition. On such nights her sleep was rife with murderers, IRA men mingling with Tontons Macoutes, the lot of them cursing and scheming in a stew of English, Irish, and rapid Creole that only she could decipher. Sometimes her Da was there; sometimes Baby Doc himself. Or Jean-Michel with his brimming sexual eyes and dark slender trunk and honed machete, his scent of smoky cooking oil. Certain souls had never abandoned her.

As usual she was awakened by bedlam in the green canopy above. For a long while she lay on her sweaty sheets listening to the cacophony of toucans and araras and howler monkeys, rude and relentless as dengue. The night had drained off some of the heat; this was the hour before the sun would become difficult, as if hurrying to scorch the land before the afternoon rains exploded. The cistern was full and she took a long, tepid shower out back, not caring if the local boys were spying on her again. For all she cared they could watch every day, revel in her shifting contours, track the daily changes in belly and breast. It was all new to her, too. They would learn together.

Back inside the cottage, her clothes were damp and smelled faintly of mildew. Nothing ever truly dried. She threw on a gauzy shift and sandals and dissected a papaya at the tiled table out back, not unhappy to be without guests, willing herself not to think about the money. Two of the treehouses needed thatching and she could not pay to do it. Meanwhile the sun dappled through the canopy deceptively. After breakfast she made a cup of coffee and took to one of the hammocks with a travel magazine someone had left behind, immersing herself in photos of Calcutta while the howlers slalomed down to steal the papaya leavings. They had a vocation. Today she did not.

At eleven she set out for the village, wanting company, intending to lunch early and get back before the rains. Paulo and Ana would be ready with soup and sausages, grilled chicken and black beans and salty *farofa*, slices of orange and pineapple and farmer's cheese. With the guests gone this early, lunch had become Maeve's ritual of coalescence, the arranging of sleep's debris into the semblance of a personality.

But as she rounded the corner she saw a familiar Land Rover parked outside, one of Moore's new men leaning against the fender and smoking a brown cigarette. A snatch of radio traffic tattered from the open window; he leaned in to take up a walkie-talkie, said a few words in patois, dropped it back in the seat. Only then did he notice the pregnant gringa making slow progress toward him in her airy shift, hazel eyes locked on his. At the sight of her he retrieved the walkie-talkie and relayed a quick report, then stepped back to clear the way.

She strode past him into the cool shadow under the thatch, a macaw flitting away, the scent of grilled meat riding the air.

"Maeve," a basso voice said from within.

She hadn't seen Xoque in months, not since she'd broken off

with Moore. It appeared he'd been upgraded, his powerful body now outfitted in a white golf shirt, immaculate khaki shorts, and expensive sandals. He might have been the doorman at a São Paulo country club, were it not for the SIG Sauer strapped to his thigh. "Not long now," he said, showing his uneven teeth and pointing to her belly.

"Counting on Lieve," she replied. Though she was no longer seeing Moore, his private doctor had promised to attend the birth. Moore was not so cruel as to stand in the way. "Lieve's still up there?"

"You're invited for lunch," said Xoque, ignoring the question.

She had no desire to see Moore again but needed to see the doctor with her own eyes. At her age she wasn't about to give birth with a native midwife. A moment later she was sitting in the rear of the Land Rover with Xoque as the driver sped them past the blockish fountain and out of town, half the village looking on.

As they approached the compound Maeve could see that something was wrong. The covered veranda was populated with valises and trunks; staff were scuttling past with furniture; Dani, the elderly carpenter, was kneeling before Moore's prized Matisse, measuring it for a crate he would build on the spot. In the gravel turnabout, the gardener was methodically smashing several computers to pieces. On the tennis court raged a bonfire heaped with documents. Moore's life was being dismantled before her eyes.

"Xoque, what's this?"

"No longer safe for Mr. Moore."

Moore had warned her once that this might happen. Someone, whether the Americans or Interpol or some new Brazilian official he hadn't yet bought off, would find him here and move in to arrest him, to break it up, whatever it was. Moore was fully prepared for that day, as was now evident. It was business.

Once inside the house, Xoque showed her to the air-conditioned dining room with its vast panoramic window overlooking the forest canopy. The room had been cleared of all furniture but the baronial table, a single chair with a silver place setting laid before it, and on the opposite wall one of Moore's most prized artworks, a

Munch lithograph of a tubercular child whose wistful gaze Maeve had always found captivating. Beside her plate sat a large manila envelope fastened with string.

As Xoque turned to go she said, "Is Moore coming?"

"Moore is gone," said Xoque. "*Pra sempre.* Forever."

Alone in the room where she'd first dined with the old man, down the long hallway from where she'd slept with him for months, Maeve sat and waited, gazing out the irresistible window. The sun had already disappeared; above the western edge of the forest a slate-grey belly of cloud glowered, gravid with the rains to come. In the course of a few minutes she saw it advance a fair distance toward the already swollen river, dipping lower as it came on, darkening the room. An erotic moment, the pause before release.

The first fit of lightning came as the cook, Neli, wheeled in a bountiful lunch of imported salmon, garden greens, white asparagus grown under lamps of Moore's own design—a faithful copy of the first meal she'd shared with Moore nearly a year before, in the aftermath of the flood. A moment later Neli returned with a chilled Riesling, filling Maeve's glass without a word.

"Neli," Maeve said.

"Senhora Kelly?"

"What's going on here?"

A look of fright crossed the youthful face. She spoke in a whisper. "Senhor Moore left in a hurry. Last night, by plane."

"Alone, Neli?"

"With the pilot and Dr. Lieve. The pilot returned this morning."

So Lieve was gone. Maeve felt the baby shift inside her.

"You'll be all right, Neli? He's provided for you somehow?"

"By the grace of God, senhora."

"Will you—" But at this moment the storm exploded over the forest with a stunning flash and a cannon shot of thunder. Both women shied from the window, joined in common reflex. Together they watched the sudden assault on the canopy, the highest tier of green buckling under the torrent. The storm rumbled through the thick window pane in a vast, slow-moving detonation, crowding the room, turning the light abruptly violet. Maeve felt the cook stop breathing. They both saw that it was no ordinary storm.

"Neli, you must go to your family. One of the men can drive

you down before the roads wash out. Should I tell Xoque?" Neli nodded quickly, plainly afraid, but whether of the storm or Xoque Maeve couldn't guess. "Fetch him, Neli. There's a good girl."

When an irritable Xoque appeared, Neli cowering behind, Maeve ordered him to get Neli and the rest of the staff to safety. "I have a *thousand* details," he protested. "Mr. Moore—"

"Moore is gone forever. You said so yourself."

"I'll send one of the men." Over his shoulder he said something harsh to Neli, who hurried off. Then, more gently, to Maeve: "You can't stay here. They're coming."

"I know. But not during this." As if in reply, the storm hurled a long, full-throated complaint against the town below. Her wineglass jittered on the table. To the east, near her own land, she saw lightning fell two palms at a blow. A cowl of mist rose from the forest floor to graze the understory.

"The pilot will take you to Moore the moment he can fly again," said Xoque, and left her to her lonely meal.

———

As Maeve grazed at her salmon she thought back to her first lunch with Moore.

"You intrigue me, Miss Kelly," he'd said, "because you've mastered the art of staying under radar. You went dark years ago and you've stayed that way. Impressive."

"You don't know anything about me."

Moore laughed broadly; she hadn't suspected he was capable of it. To her right, the Dutch doctor studied her plate. "That's not exactly true, Miss Kelly. My sources are better than most. Though you were a challenge for us, I'll admit." He sipped his wine, let this sink in. "By the way, may I call you Miss Flanagan, just for the sake of accuracy?"

Maeve waited to see what else he had.

"Alright, then, what do we know? Mary Flanagan, born in Derry two years after her brother Rodney, parents good Catholics. Fled with the family to Belfast after the Bogside riot—perhaps a poor choice. Within a year her father's in deep with the Provos, a first-class provocateur. An assassin, actually. How am I doing so far?"

For once she was speechless. By whatever means, he'd traced a decades-long trail backward from a Brazilian rainforest to her murderous homeland. She thought of the satellite dishes clustered on the roof, imagined an invisible flow of damning intelligence coursing through them to a screen somewhere in the rambling house. She set her fork down and said nothing, a runnel of sweat wandering down her back despite the air conditioning. Moore went on.

"Next comes a particularly heinous hit—a clergyman in mufti, a noncombatant. A serious error. Mary's brother Roddy is arrested, but her father escapes to a safe house with two mates. They wait it out. The heat begins to subside—Roddy's made an example of—and then something odd happens, something I'll confess I don't yet understand."

The Dutch doctor and Moore looked over at Maeve in perfect synchrony. A mute server slipped in to refill her glass, withdrew. The rains would soon trundle in. Even from Moore's redoubt Maeve could sense the anxiety down in the town, the memory of the flood stirring. There was a world outside the room and she would have liked to escape into it, but Moore's data held her rapt.

"Perhaps," said Moore, "you can help me understand how a fugitive IRA hit man turns up in Haiti as adviser to Baby Doc? His teenage daughter in tow?"

It was not for him to know—not yet.

She'd been a girl of sixteen, a virgin with a loaded Webley tucked under her mattress, when her father or brother, it didn't matter which, shot a Reverend James. She was seventeen when, under cover of darkness, she and her Da shoved off from the Bannock Cove, to be intercepted some hours later by a trawler with no running lights, while her Ma stayed behind to pine for Roddy's acquittal. By unlucky timing she was in the grip of brutal menstrual cramps and then the flu and so would barely recall the rough passage on the cargo freighter, the hold killingly hot as the ship transected the Atlantic and plied southward. The day came when her Da called her onto the blazing deck and they watched the freighter make its ponderous landfall in Haiti, a country she couldn't have found on a map.

She'd never seen a black man in her life. Now her Da would be working for one—not just any black man, but one anointed President for Life, a blustering connoisseur of killers who'd admired the IRA's handiwork from afar. None of which she'd fully understand until the evening when she lay half-hidden in the vetiver with Jean-Michel, her very own winsome killer, and teased his rose nipple with the tip of his machete until he told her the truth. By then Da was famous among the Tontons, *Irishman nan fou*, the crazy Irishman. Her lover was in awe of him. It made her proud. Only later, after a report of Tontons eating the raw heart of a girl exactly her age in Gonaïves, did the grit of it make her flee.

This much she would eventually tell Moore, late one night in his lavish bedroom under the softly watchful eye of a Degas dancer. A bottle of Margaux sped her along, and her lover's rapt attention as well: she felt his admiration, one canny fugitive's for another. Day by day she was taming him, this rough, unhandsome American with expensive tastes, and it excited her. She could not deny it. That he would not say what his business was or where his money came from would have troubled a different sort of woman, but she, more than anyone, understood the value of secrets. She stood with him on the veranda and shot monkeys out of the jacarandas with his Widowmaker, all of it coming back to her in an electric surge.

Yet she would not stay with him for more than a night at a time. It was a matter of principle, and she had a business to run, guests to tend to. Rubem, the manager he'd hired for her, panicked easily when problems arose, when an American collapsed with heat stroke or the water supply was obstructed by a dead macaque. And so Xoque and a driver—eventually just Xoque—would spirit her back into town, into her own world, leaving Moore on his red hill to observe her withdrawal through the U-boat gunner's scope mounted to the balcony railing.

In the empty dining room of Moore's empty house she abandons her salmon and Riesling, tasting nothing, unable to take her gaze off the worsening storm. The rain is torrential now. The river will soon make a lunge for the town, rushing in through gullies carved by last year's flood in disastrous and raging flumes. Against this rain the new levee, really just a low wall of leaking sandbags, will be worthless. She imagines Paulo and Ana standing in the swamped ruins of Casa Ribeiro; then the elderly Nogueiras, lame and demented, consumed by the swirling brown waters. Infants will be carried off, swallowed. Maeve pictures her own home lifted off its foundations and sent barging down the riotous estuary. Yet in Moore's aerie all is calm and abstract. She gazes into the storm like a diver inspecting a vast wall of coral, in no hurry to surface, Munch's dying girl looking on with her.

Neli doesn't come to remove her dishes—a sign that, with luck, she's been driven home by one of the men. Whatever is happening down in the town, she should be with her kin. Maeve pushes her plate away and takes up the manila envelope beside it, unwinding the string from the clasp, wondering who's still at large in the echoing house.

Moore has left her the briefest of farewell notes, clipped to a printout filled with rows of numbers.

Maeve, I've had to leave.

Join me—it may not be safe for you there, given our association. João will fly you out discreetly. I make this offer in earnest.

But knowing you, you'll refuse. If so, please accept the attached as a parting gift—something to help you get by, and the town too, if you like. The Munch you love is yours for the taking. But I do hope you'll come.

— Moore.

On the printout he's scrawled, *Each of these should be good for 30 days after first use. Clean and untraceable. The accounts clear offshore, then route to yours; they can't find you.*

She puzzles over the thicket of digits for a moment before realizing that they are credit card numbers, dozens of them. It sorts quickly in her mind: the uplink, the computers, the priceless artwork, and wines. She stares at the pages, then at the green cataclysm on the other side of the window, then at the pages once again, and she slips them back in their envelope.

"Xoque!" she calls down the echoing hallway, and while she's waiting for him she lifts the Munch from its hook, the envelope tucked under her arm.

From her vantage point in Treetop Lodge 2 she can see it all. The brown, muscular arm of the river sweeping across the water-logged land, goats and dogs and smashed furniture riding it like flies on a horse's flank. To the east, her inundated town, a yard of putrid water standing in the internet café, in the old hotel, in Ribeiro's restaurant, the ruination general now. The memorial fountain in the square half-submerged but still, with pointless bravery, shooting a streamer of water up through the deluge. Silver piranhas cascading into the small colonial chapel, the newer graves threatening to leach open in the churchyard. Shirtless men in rowboats navigating new waterways. Produce streaming from the greengrocer's: passionfruit and collards and bruised papaya carried off by the current. An uprooted palm fanning its panicked fingers as it passes. Even from her perch she can hear the roar of the water.

On the roof of the workers' quarters behind the hotel, families have rigged tarps and lean-tos, settling in, the women cooking drowned chickens and a monkey on a makeshift brazier.

She's seen enough. Cradling her belly from below, she crosses to where Xoque sits on the treehouse floor smoking, his yellow eyes half-lidded, his smooth chest shining with perspiration. Maeve lowers herself carefully to the cool bamboo planks and leans back between his raised knees, settling against his body, his cigarette smoke suspended above. Without a word Xoque shapes a broad palm to her huge belly as if to comfort the child within. Eventually Maeve falls into a dreamless sleep, the emptiness blessed and oceanic, while above them the rain sways in curtains tall as the coastal mountains, shimmering in the contrary sunlight, heavy with life.

Night
in
Erg
Chebbi

In July, seven months to the day after her brother's death, they arrive in Merzouga, Morocco, gateway to the dune sea of Erg Chebbi. The trip is meant to be a healing interlude, a brief escape: by immersing her in this place of exotic sights and sounds he has hoped to give her a short respite from her grief. But everything has gone wrong—a missed connection in Frankfurt, his billfold stolen in a Casablanca hamam, a bout of diarrhea that kept them from enjoying the lavish riad in Essaouira. The grinding logistics of travel have steadily overwhelmed their interest in their surroundings. Now, in the sand-blown streets of this tenuous little Saharan town, its mud-brick houses strung together with exposed electrical wires, they have lost the energy to keep talking. For more than an hour they've walked in the killing heat without exchanging a word. Even the effort of silence is draining.

They pass a horse cart carrying four women in black burkhas, jumbled against one another like quarry rocks. Earlier in the trip they would have taken a furtive snapshot of the scene, but it no longer matters. The bucking road trip from Erfoud has defeated them, and the heat that permeates everything, and the extreme dryness of the air, and the blackflies that seek out the eyes for the meager moisture they offer. Eventually they head back to the hotel, shut themselves in their spartan room with the clattering air conditioner turned high, and fall asleep in their separate beds.

When the phone jangles to announce the departure of the overnight excursion into the dunes they wash quickly, zip up their bags, and head down to the lobby to meet the driver, a gloomy young man in camouflage pants, a Michael Jackson teeshirt and a burnoose.

Desert? he asks by way of identifying himself, and Wilson nods, extending a hand which the man ignores. Hassan, he says brusquely, and the formalities are concluded.

Aren't those American-issue? Anna asks the driver, pointing to the desert-toned camouflage pants, but he either has no English or pretends he hasn't. Hassan heaves their bags into the back of a dented Jeep and a moment later they set off down the rutted piste, passing through the cracked keyhole of the town gate, portal to the Sahara. The radio blares out a caustic blend of heavy metal and Bedouin keening until Wilson leans forward and covers his ears to ask that it be turned off. The rest of the trip will pass in hostile silence, the driver taking every opportunity to harry plodding camels and carts and the occasional decrepit Fiat.

———

They are heading straight into the desert and the scenery unfolding before them is spectacular—the setting sun throwing long shadows out from every dimple in the sand, the endless smooth flanks of the Sahara taking on the look of a woman's body—but the driver's anger makes it impossible to focus on what isn't within the Jeep's impact zone.

You shouldn't have provoked him, Anna tells Wilson, looking back out the dusty window.

A few miles outside Merzouga they pass the body of a juvenile camel festering by the roadside, dogs and blackflies bickering over the remains. Anna pivots in her seat to track it as they drive past.

Takes the art of roadkill to a whole new level, she says, perhaps intending humor, perhaps not—it is hard to tell with her lately. A few more miles reel by; she rummages in her shoulder bag and comes up with the bottle of *mahia* they've brought from the hotel. In just two weeks she's developed a passion for the date-anise spirits, and the flask with its ornate label is never far from her hand. She takes a deep swallow and offers the bottle to Wilson as an afterthought. He demurs, stomach shaken by the ride. Soon after, the road collapses into a sketchy trail, little more than a scratch across the desert, and the Jeep slows as its fat wheels grind through the sand.

At a certain point Wilson becomes aware that they are being watched, and meets Hassan's grey eyes in the mirror. The driver should be watching the way ahead, but he has been watching them—more specifically, watching the American woman drinking straight from the bottle in the rear seat. Wilson widens his eyes slightly, sending a question forward, but Hassan merely looks away, punching the accelerator as if to make a point. When the Jeep bucks, the bottle snaps forward and a splash of mahia is lost. *Shit!* she snaps, but the driver lays into his horn for no apparent reason and her complaint is lost in the unruly commotion of the late afternoon.

By the time they reach the camp the light is failing, the towering dunes indistinct but massive, the atmosphere fading from brick red to faint blue. The land has cooled suddenly and there is a tang of smoke on the air. As they approach they see a play of torches throwing shadows on a cluster of Bedouin tents, the squat forms of camels hunkered down at the edge of the camp. When Hassan kills the engine, a rataplan of drums rolls out to meet them with what they assume to be a traditional greeting; they search the dusk for the drummers and discover that it's just a tape player hooked to a car battery. The drumming stops abruptly and it is instantly silent, the desert vast enough to absorb all sound. But then there is a tinkle of crude bells: tan and white baby goats arrive and scuffle around the Jeep, making childish noises.

I hope you aren't dinner, Anna tells the animals.

Over there, snaps Hassan, pointing toward the largest tent, and they are handed off to a turbaned, long-faced man in scarlet regalia who introduces himself as Tahnoon, a sheikh of the Bani Kinanah. Wilson tips the driver, guessing at the right amount and then halving it, and nervously consigns their bags to two boys who are smiling a bit too energetically. They have arrived.

Within the hour they have taken tea in Tahnoon's tent—a bit of bad theater involving weak mint *atay* served by a grim, sweating girl in stained harem pants—and are installed in their own, a bivouac filled with tribal rugs and pillows, a hammered-brass tea table, a dented hookah, and plastic-covered twin mattresses that might have come from a Sears warehouse in Ohio. At the sight of these Anna and Wilson catch each other's eye and smile tiredly. The trip is beginning to take on an absurd edge that will, with luck, be its charm when they relive it later.

Blankets, says Anna. Find blankets. Mind the lice and scorpions.

As he leaves the tent she takes out the bottle of mahia and places it on the low table, settling in. He roves the small camp, comes upon the servant girl, and manages to communicate his request through sign language and broken French, hoping she does not misunderstand his intentions when he pantomimes the act of lying down. As he returns to the tent, crossing between tall torches thrust into the sand, he decides not to tell Anna about the two baby goats roasting on spits behind a makeshift rug curtain.

There do not appear to be any other guests in the camp. The other three sleeping tents are empty, their door flaps tied back. Since arriving, they've seen only the sheikh, the driver, the servant girl, the bag boys, and one or two other staff. Presumably a cook or two are working behind their blind, but there is no sign of any foreigners other than themselves. Tagines steam over a low charcoal fire and the scent of cinnamon-spiced meat fills the crisp air. Against the radiance of the torches the dunes are just shapeless giants somewhere out in the indistinct night. One of the boys reappears with an oudh and sits down crosslegged next to the fire pit, beginning to pick out a wandering melody with surprising skill. Dinner is laid out on rugs. Wilson knows it's goat but tells her it's lamb. The sheikh directs them to their cushions with a grand gesture, and as they get settled a vision appears from the shadows, or perhaps it is from a distant past: they make out a dark, lanky man costumed as some sort of Zouave soldier, complete with ballooning red trousers, sash, tasseled fez, and blue brocade jacket. He lurks at the edge of the firelight with an automatic rifle cradled in his arms, apparently to stand guard over the proceedings. The costume might date from the Crimean War, but the assault weapon is real enough. Morocco is supposed to be safe and at peace, but it is impossible to look at the weapon and not think of tribal militias, bandits, rebels, jihadis, desert fighters with nothing to lose. The evening takes on an unwonted gravity, a strange density, as the rifle and its keeper lurk in the half-light.

While they dine, the sheikh expounds on Bedouin culture in an English that is three parts American television and one part phrasebook, then begins asking them bluntly personal questions. How big is their house? Are their families rich? When he asks why they don't have children and then asks twice more, not satisfied with their vague answers, Anna pointedly turns away, suddenly entranced by the oudh. The sheikh lets it go and lights a hookah, smoking noisily and staring at her with no effort to conceal his pique. All the while the costumed guard stands close by, weapon at the ready.

After dinner and sticky sweets they decide to retire early, washing and relieving themselves in the convenience tent, as the sheikh calls it. Their host manages a brief show of obsequious courtesy and the awkward evening is over at last. As Wilson ties the tent flap behind him he catches a glimpse of the driver Hassan and the servant girl, who has exchanged her harem costume for tight jeans and a fake leather jacket: they climb into the Jeep and churn away into the night, headlights off, a ghost ship trawling a dark sea.

Night in Erg Chebbi   19

Someone has lit an oil lamp on the low table and the interior of the tent glows warmly. Anna puts it out immediately, casting everything into darkness.

I liked the lamp, Wilson says.

They put that there hoping for a strip show, can't you see? To put the Western lady on stage.

She busies herself smoothing a scratchy blanket over one of the mattresses, making up a pallet, while he lounges and listens, taking in the woolly smell of the place. Anna is too preoccupied to notice such details. She has gained some weight since her brother Danny's death; he finds it attractive but she hates herself for it. It has given her a perpetually nervous edge. Eventually he hears her settle on her mattress, then hears her ease out the cork of the mahia bottle.

We could push the mattresses together, he says to the darkness.

The blankets won't fit. Too small.

So what? We'll make it work. I would like to sleep with my wife again someday.

This freezes her, her busy nest-making abruptly stilled. In the absolute darkness he pictures her kneeling beside the mattress, uncertain how to respond. Finally she says:

Would you, Wilson? Want to sleep with me?

I miss you, Anna.

I do too, she says faintly, and then she is on his mattress with him, her arms around his neck, the Sahara slumbering just beyond the walls of the tent. Her breath is heavy with the anise of the mahia; her hair smells of smoke and meat and sand. But there is no one more familiar to him than the woman in his arms.

After receiving news of Danny's death seven months before, she had pitched camp in the darkness of the basement guest room. He stayed with her for several nights but eventually moved back up to the master bedroom, finding her grief impenetrable; she would not allow him to console her or even touch her, rebuffing his every approach. She told him again and again to leave her alone, and eventually he decided he should do so. He would kiss her impassive face, ask her if there was anything she needed, and head upstairs through the silent house, deeply worried for her yet also relieved to escape the dark field of her grief.

But even as the initial shock began to ease, as she began to talk to him about Danny, she said she preferred to spend her nights downstairs. She gave various reasons—the firm mattress, the coziness of the room, the quiet—but it slowly became obvious that she no longer wished to sleep with him. And so they drifted into sleeping apart. He raised it with her more than once, pleading with her to tell him what was wrong, but she held doggedly to her implausible reasons, leaving them at an impasse. It was on the eve of the Morocco trip that he finally confronted her outright and she admitted it: since her brother's death she could not imagine herself making love to him. It wasn't about him; she had tried to masturbate more than once, but her sexuality was simply absent—vanished. She felt nothing at all.

She didn't understand what was wrong. It made no sense that the two things would be connected, but somehow in her heart they were. It had all ended in tears, an unimpeachable anguish on her part, and he had let it be. Neither of them needed to say that they hoped Morocco might give them the breakthrough they needed.

And so now, as she slips a chapped hand beneath his shirt and begins to stroke his chest, he is excited and afraid at the same time. They have not made love since the Christmas before Danny's passing, have barely kissed. Her hands explore his body as if they are sleeping together for the first time, and suddenly he finds himself urgently aroused. They are out of their clothes in a heartbeat and he reclaims his place in the great hush of the desert, not caring what the rest of the camp might hear.

When it's done they lie in each other's arms, exhausted and profoundly relieved, listening to the small sounds of the camp being buttoned down for the night. The camels are fussing at the edge of the sea of dunes, chuttering at one another in the darkness. Somewhere a pot bangs, is silenced. He picks up the scent of a cigarette, strong enough to be just outside the tent, but in the next moment falls into a heavy sleep, *la petite mort* overtaking him. It's possible that she is crying when he drifts off; he can't be sure, and can't stay awake long enough to investigate further.

Sometime later, perhaps deep in the night, he is roused by the sound of voices. One is hers, and he hears a brittleness in it that worries him. The other voice is indistinct, but he soon realizes, by process of elimination, that it must be the Zouave guard's. Easing back the tent flap, he sees his wife sitting crosslegged under a blanket at the edge of the firelight, smoking with the Zouave as they stare into the black desert, the guard's assault rifle resting casually in his lap. He sits apart from her at a respectful distance, an act of courtesy that forces her to speak more loudly than the setting might call for. The bottle of mahia sitting beside her in the sand may also have something to do with it. He wonders how long she's been up drinking. When she speaks again he hears the slur in her voice.

—on his last day of leave, damn it. What kind of assholes would put him on a plane back to Afghanistan the day after Christmas?

Very good, madame, says the Zouave.

There is a long pause. Wilson sees her exhale a spool of cigarette smoke, then look over at the Zouave as if to size him up.

What the hell kind of uniform is that, anyway?

Very good, madame.

Did the circus come after you when you ran off? That why you have the gun?

Yes, madame, the guard says uncertainly. Anna laughs roughly at her own joke and coughs into the night.

Guess your English isn't any better than my Arabic.

Anna watches the Zouave and Wilson watches the pair of them. The Zouave pulls his knees up to his chest, discomfited by the American woman's unflinching stare. Wilson has a bad feeling about what's going on and considers leaving the tent, interceding in some way, but she begins to speak again and he can't afford to miss a word. Her voice falls now and he can barely make out what she's saying.

Danny spoke Arabic, she says. Spoke it fluently. They had him as an interpreter when they'd go into villages. He was the one'd calm everyone down, pave the way, bridge the gap. You know? Build trust because he spoke the language. My little brother was the only kid in our high school that took French *and* German *and* Spanish. Smarter than you and me put together. Why he joined the Army is beyond me. He could have done anything. We all thought so.

Very good, madame.

It wasn't good at all. It was dead stupid. We were already in Afghanistan and he has to go and join the fucking Army.

The Zouave watches her carefully, hearing the change in her tone even across the chasm of language and culture. He says nothing now; she is really talking to herself anyway.

I'll tell you something, when I opened that door on Christmas Day and saw him standing there in camouflage fatigues it just brought it all home to me, brought the whole fucked-up situation down on my head. All of a sudden I went, like, *political*. What, was he proud of himself to show up for Christmas dinner in camouflage? At his own sister's house in Kearney, Nebraska? *Merry Christmas, Anna Banana!* he says, and hands me this half-frozen scarlet poinsettia. And you know what I say back?

The Zouave watches impassively as she answers her own question:

Don't you wear fucking camouflage into my house if you want to get fed.

That's what his bitchy big sister says to him as he stands there in the cold with his hopeful red face. I remember him tilting his head to make sure he heard me right—he'd been wearing a hearing aid since an IED blew his eardrum out. He tilted his head and in that moment it reminded me of this German shepherd we grew up with, Rudy, and for some reason that's what broke my heart. But I didn't show my heart to him. I just closed the door and sent my own brother away from Christmas dinner, sent him out into a Nebraska snowstorm with his frozen poinsettia in his frozen hands, twelve hours before he shipped back to the kill zone. What kind of a person would do that?

She stops as if expecting an answer from the Zouave, but the tall man has retracted into himself now, his long limbs folded neatly against his blue brocade uniform jacket, his turbaned head on his knee. Wilson thinks he sees Anna nod as if acknowledging a response that has not come. She takes a long pull from the mahia bottle and continues:

My poor husband's out picking up the wine while all this happens—to this day he doesn't know what I did to my little brother. I've never told anyone. *Danny must be running late,* he says when he gets home. *Must be the lousy weather.* And I don't take that opportunity to correct him. I owe it to him to tell the truth, but I can't. I owe it to Danny, too.

So Danny's gone and we sit a long time drinking red wine and finally we eat just the two of us, and I have to pretend I don't know what happened. I actually have no idea where Danny is or how to reach out to him. We'd only talked once since he got back and he didn't say where he was staying this time. But I knew he sure wouldn't be back for dinner. He'd killed people over there, but what I said hurt him just like he was a little kid. I saw the little boy in him that night, the boy with freezing cold hands and a frozen fucking houseplant and a sister who'd just thrown him out on Christmas night. A heartbroken kid is what I saw.

So by now Wilson's pushing me to call the police about Danny. The snow is nasty and he's afraid Danny's been in a wreck. I start to wonder too. Fortunately for me the phone rings and it's a telemarketer but I pretend it's my brother, I carry on this whole imaginary conversation saying I'm sorry he's got the flu and feel better and so on, and when I hang up the phone I look Wilson right in the eye and repeat the whole lie. *Improve* on it. Say Danny's pissed because they'll make him ship out even though he's been puking his guts up, et cetera. I just bald-face lie to my husband and pour us both another glass of wine. I think about Danny's frozen red poinsettia and it's all I can do to hold it together.

Hm, says the guard, nodding in his turban as the agitated American lady blows smoke into the dunes. Suddenly she stands, flicks the cigarette into the sand and buries it with her bare foot. She raises her voice, speaking not to the guard now but to the open desert.

And then they fucking kill him. Ten days later he's on patrol in Helmand and some kids lure my brother Danny into a Taliban ambush and they grab his service pistol and shoot him in the head, like a Mafia hit. They *execute* my little brother with his own weapon behind some fucking mud hut. I'm sure he's wearing that same camouflage and I'm sure that's part of what gets him killed. It gets him kicked out of his sister's house on Christmas and then it gets him killed on the other side of the world.

<hr>

Anna pauses to catch her breath, then steps toward the dunes, passing beyond the firelight's ambit. Her edges waver in the murk; the volume of her body becomes indefinite. All at once she is half apparition, half mortal.

Madame! says the Zouave anxiously, scrambling to his feet, sensing that something is wrong but lacking the English to comprehend what it might be. The American lady is sobbing now, clawing her fingers through her hair, and the blanket drops to the sand, abruptly revealing her ghostly nakedness. She turns and steps back into the circle of firelight, her breasts and belly and sex on full display. Instinctively the guard reaches for the blanket and drapes it around her, then turns his back modestly. She makes no effort to secure the blanket and it falls to the ground again.

Anna notices that the Zouave has left his rifle on the sand. She stoops to take it and turns back toward the invisible dunes. The guard is still turned away, averting his eyes, unaware that she has taken up his weapon.

When Wilson sees his wife direct the barrel of the rifle upward toward her own face he bursts from the tent and runs to her, crossing the encampment in five bounds. At the sound of his steps she pivots to confront him, the rifle awkward in her arms, her face contorted. When she sees it's him she begins to move away, retreating into the open hand of the desert.

Anna! he shouts. The Zouave is at his side now, the two of them watching the vanishing woman in her nakedness. She begins to sob compulsively, disintegrating, losing control in a hot cascade of tears.

You should leave me, Wilson, she calls out in a choked voice.

He begins to walk toward her but stops when she lowers the rifle and shakily targets the Zouave at his side. The tall man says something in Arabic, perhaps a prayer, perhaps a curse. Together they watch her struggle through the deep sand, dragging herself backward, a white cloud dissipating into the dunes. Eventually she stumbles against a low hillock and glances over her shoulder, then turns to scramble up and over it. Only her head and shoulders remain in view, the rifle hidden by the dunes. In another moment she has vanished completely.

Wilson bolts from the torchlight toward the place where she disappeared. It is freezing in the desert—he's wearing nothing but pajama bottoms—and he can no longer see the sand at his feet. The moon has long since set and the stars are gauzed over with cloud, or perhaps a distant dust storm. He labors forward like a man lost in a catacomb.

Anna! he calls, already winded by the sand's resistance. Anna!

Right here, Wilson.

Her voice is startlingly close, just off to his right at ground level. She must be sitting in the sand.

Where are you? He extends his hand in the darkness, probing for her, scenting her.

Stay where you are, Wilson.

Anna, he pleads, just let me sit with you.

In the distance he hears a commotion brewing, sounds of voices and brisk activity, but the space between them is very still.

Wilson, my love, I think I have to leave you.

Her voice is calmer now, burred with the liquor. He drops to the sand, drawing his knees up against the cold. He judges that she is not more than ten feet away.

What do you mean, leave me? he pleads. What have I done?

You've done everything right, Wilson. Everything. I don't deserve you. That's why I have to leave. There are things you don't know. Things I've done that disgust me. I'm not fit to be with anyone.

He thinks he hears a metallic sound, a meshing of metal parts, but the sound is indistinct.

Anna, he continues, his mind racing, but then a terrifying burst of gunfire breaks out, deafening and brutally physical at such close range. On reflex he rolls onto the sand. In the next instant a blinding electric light snaps on from the dune above and reveals his naked wife kneeling very close by, her back to him, the squat assault rifle in her arms. The weapon is in firing position. Another burst of gunfire rips through the desert's emptiness as she shoots into the empty dunes in a haphazard figure-eight, sending up tiny explosions of sand in the harsh electric light. She screams as she shoots, and when the shooting stops she screams still louder, the sharp peal of her pain careening out into the Sahara like a raven hurled from a sandstorm.

The electric light snaps off as suddenly as it snapped on, and all is once again in darkness. Wilson is afraid to approach her, uncertain what she will do next, uncertain of the source of the bright light. Blinded, he feels threats on all sides. His ears are still ringing from the salvo.

Then the light reappears and he sees his wife laid out before him. She lies face down in the sand, thick hair fanned across the desert floor, one leg hitched up as if frozen in flight. He thinks of Pompeii, of the stricken bodies. No blood is visible; Anna's muscular back heaves in the harsh light, her breathing fast and rough. The assault rifle lies discarded in the sand a few yards away from her. All this Wilson absorbs at a glance, trying to make sense of the scene before him.

From atop the adjacent dune, a snort and a spit announce the presence of a camel. The rider sweeps the odd scene with a powerful handheld spotlight, lingering on the American woman's ghostly white skin, the arc of her body, her splayed leg. Behind the blinding beam Wilson can just make out the sheikh on his mount and the Zouave standing beside the huge animal. The two men exchange words in Arabic and the sheikh laughs mirthlessly, sitting back in his rug saddle and toying with the reins. His camel stamps the sand and tosses its head in irritation, eager to get back to camp, its pruney scent rolling down the slope of the dune. Then the spotlight snaps off again and the desert closes in suddenly. The Zouave moves effortlessly through the complete darkness and retrieves the discarded rifle, the sound of its swinging strap the only indication that he has taken it. With a dismissive snort the camel lumbers down the far side of the dune, the Zouave presumably following, and Anna and Wilson are alone in the desert, shipwrecked on an invisible sea.

Wilson feels his way across the dune toward Anna and comes

upon her soft thigh, a thing of great delicacy next to the gritty sand. He lies down beside his wife and embraces her in the impenetrable Moroccan night, the two of them shivering in the cold, her nails digging into his back. When they get to their feet some time later the sky has cleared and the firmament above is exploding with stars, a celestial firestorm as suffocating as it is beautiful. Though they are freezing—though the hulking dunes, visible again in the starlight, are terrifying in their mass—they stop and look upward, unable to ignore the spectacle above.

Take me home, Wilson, Anna says quietly. I think all these stars might kill me.

Light Year

Anne Sweigart sits in a Cleveland diner crowded with grim truckers and Elvis memorabilia, gazing down upon the sort of breakfast she hasn't allowed herself in years. After one look at the heaping platter she caps her drafting pen and calls for more coffee, knowing she'll need the extra lift just to gut it out. In her long career as a photojournalist Anne has eaten in every manner of dubious establishment, from bullet-riddled falafel shops in Gaza to filthy noodle barges plying the Mekong River, but while in the States she's always followed a stricter regimen. She has preferred to cook for herself and dine alone, to exert total control over what enters her body. Nothing fried; no dessert other than fruit;

red meat in sparing doses only. It has been her way of girding for the next assignment. Having sweat out malaria in back-country Afghanistan and dengue fever in Dakar, she's known for years that physical preparation is key to her success and, on occasion, her survival.

Yet now she faces a ziggurat of pancakes slicked with syrup and buttressed by four stout sausage links, the whole pile glistening with menacing appeal under the green billiard lamp above. This childish breakfast would have been an abomination to her a year ago, but now she finds she can forgive herself such indulgences. Perhaps it is the years of subsisting on rice and lentils and gristly goat, on curries of suspect provenance and fruit gathered from chicken yards behind roadside squats, but she has decided that she will eat as she pleases and give it no further thought.

And so Anne carefully removes her thick glasses, puts away the printout of climatological statistics and begins her solitary breakfast, the featureless white morning sky entirely consistent with her program for the day.

———————

Down by the lake it is bitterly cold, as cold as any day she's endured in Khost or Lhasa or Baffin Bay. Her hands ache with arthritis as she unzips her camera case and splays the legs of the heavy tripod. She has already chosen her vantage point, having reconnoitered the dismal shoreline the morning before like a soldier walking the ramparts, assessing fortifications, looking for points of exposure. She is very interested in exposure, as it happens, but of a different sort: it is all about the light now. The grey scalp of the water; the cold phosphorescence of cirrus clouds as the sun lurks behind them; the slow reefs of ice that slide through a spectrum of bony whites as the morning inches forward. She is interested too in the absence of light—in the harsh way that a glowing cloud, for example, is bisected by the dark rule of a smokestack. In the crevices beneath the tumbled breakwater rocks it is as black as a starless night. All this she knows at a glance.

She shoots a hundred pictures quickly, then leans back on a frigid rock to smoke a cigarette, killing time while the light evolves.

There is nothing of traditional photographic interest here, but she has not come to Cleveland to create a thing of beauty or to render social commentary. If she juxtaposes a factory's smokestacks with the glazed face of Lake Erie, it is only to register a particular flux of light. She needs this datum, this observation, just as in an earlier time she would have sought out the face of a particular child as a window into a war. The fragment reveals the whole. She holds a bundle of smoke in her lungs, mostly for the warmth of it, and wonders whether the bone-deep pain in her right wrist might hint at a larger pain. The fragment, the whole. Exhaling with a burst, she nods at her taxi driver, who idles nearby chattering on a cell phone in some East African tongue—Somali, she thinks.

Her approach to her art has always been holographic. Her most famous picture, the picture that won her a Pulitzer, focused on the smoke unfurling from an exhausted firefighter's cigarette as he prepared himself to go back into the smoking Ground Zero pile. The cigarette's tiny plume said everything about the huge cowl that overhung the death scene in the deep field of the photograph. She no longer likes the photo—there is a whiff of Schadenfreude about it—but she does recognize her signature in the composition, the universal concealed in the weft of the particular.

The French love this about her work. Floating somewhere in a bottom drawer of her life there is a reprint of an article by the French critic Dufour, who long ago convinced himself that her work is based on the mathematical theory of fractals—another system, she has learned, in which the part stands for the whole. It is ridiculous, of course, and all the more so because Dufour has never contacted her to ask in plain terms whether his hunch is correct.

A long rill of cloud is beginning to take on an umber edge, possibly just a pollution effect but a variant that interests her nevertheless. She stubs out her cigarette on the stone breakwater and gets back to work, locking the camera upward like a telescope, targeting the open sky. A wind is kicking up over a dirty ice floe on the lake; she gathers her collar against her neck, calculating her settings, thinking it through in the new way. The old instincts no longer apply, because making classically correct photographs is no longer the point. With a few turns of the camera wheel she dials in her aperture and begins to shoot, clicking the remote methodically in the harsh wind.

The close study of light is enough to reveal everything of interest to her now. Faces, steel or stone edifices, bodies of water are useful only as its interpreters, translators of the sun's patois. She has chosen Cleveland as her first stop because it averages only nine days of sun from December through February. It is the death of light. The shots she takes here will give her a baseline, the narrowest possible spectral band against which all other landscapes might be judged. The perpetual gloaming of this tired city is the dark matter that reveals itself by perturbing the space around it, expressing itself much as she does.

In the evening, on the airplane, the crew dims the lights and suddenly her visual field contracts to the diameter of a salad plate. There is nothing before her but the tiny television screen with its commotion of chattering faces, hectic graphics, parodies of war: once again her world has narrowed intolerably. Only by turning her head might she be sure that she is not alone in the cabin.

Her peripheral vision has been worsening over these last weeks, outpaced only by the total collapse of her night vision. Without ambient light her eyesight all but vanishes. She is staring down a dark tunnel into a dark night, unable to register whether she is an inch or a mile from the walls that enclose her.

With the fading of her eyesight, her feeling for exposure has changed. She began to pay serious attention to her failing vision, in fact, only when she noticed that she was nudging her apertures wider, shooting at f/5.6 or f/4 in situations where her instinct might have been f/8. Her shutter speeds were slowing too. She needed to let more light in: when shot with her old techniques the photos felt dull and lifeless, even on the bright display screen at the studio. For a run of terrible months she puzzled with rising anxiety over her errors—for this is what they seemed to be when she inspected her work—worried that her judgment was slipping.

But the fact was, she had been a professional photographer for thirty-five years; she could not have forgotten all that she once knew. It took time for her to realize that she was simply compensating, unconsciously, for a decline in her eyesight. The problem was not in the shooting, but in the eye of the beholder.

That spring, at the insistence of her friend Darra, she saw an ophthalmologist in Brooklyn and learned that she was suffering from the same degenerative disease that had blinded her mother at forty-two. It seemed that a tiny defect in her rods and cones was destroying her ability to do what she loved most. She knew without being told—knew as an article of primitive belief—that there would be no cure. It was not about the science, which had surely advanced since her mother's day; it was simply a circle closing. Long ago she'd realized that her drive to become a photographer had begun with her mother's blindness, with those afternoons when the two of them would sit in the garden and she would describe the roses to her, the salmon petals, speckled canes, leaves the green of gunpowder tea. This is where it had begun, and this is where it would now end, the blind leading the blind.

Educate me, she told the doctor. But keep it short.

That night Darra tried to seduce her, then made do with listening from the depths of an armchair while she talked nonstop about her work, her plans and projects, the large-format camera she'd been enlisted to test for Nikon, the possibility of embedding with an Army Ranger unit in Mosul. It was as if nothing had happened.

Anne, said Darra eventually in his neutral voice. Everything changes now. You should think about the places you want to see while you still have your sight.

She liked him, to the degree that she did, for just this factual plainness. But in the moment she was unable to bear it. She gathered her things and was back on the subway in under fifteen minutes. Over the next three hours she smoked an entire pack of cigarettes, tipping open the hotel window and exhaling into the blurry night. The lights of Manhattan flared beneath her, but her memory told her more of the cityscape below than her eyes could. It was like being stopped in mid-descent while losing consciousness, the world half-filled with blackness, the mind half-swallowed.

Anne wore her clothes to bed that night and dreamed of nothing and no one, the day a total loss. Upon waking it took her a long time to recall what had happened, and this delayed reaction gave her some strength, as if her diagnosis were not the central fact of her life. Only later, as the sun escaped and the light around her faded with its new suddenness, did she allow herself to collapse, drawing a bath and drinking room service whiskey until she fell into a leaden sleep. She awoke some hours later still drunk and chilled to the bone, the bath gone cold, and threw on all the lights, inspecting her gaunt body in the bathroom mirror as she slaked the water from it. Her fallen breasts were indistinct mounds, her pubis a dark smudge, the scar from her gall bladder surgery a faint white comma: soon she would lose the ability to take her own measure, to discern her own anatomy.

―――――――

Anne Sweigart could not have said which was more distressing, losing her eyesight or losing her art. It was an impossible choice—a cruelty—and in the last analysis the two things were one and the same.

Her diagnosis had come while she was off assignment for a rare stretch, the magazine that was her usual outlet having been acquired by a company with more interest in paparazzi than photojournalists. The summer gaped before her. She did not know quite what to do with her pain, which at times edged into desperation, an emotion she knew mostly from observing others. And so she installed herself at the family summer house up in Alberta, spending whole days in silence, smoking before the prim little lake and trying to think her way through her situation. At dusk she would switch on a halogen lamp and write down whatever she had learned that day, then would cook a gradual dinner, listening to Shostakovich or Górecki and pausing at intervals to top off her scotch and write some more. In the evenings she felt a sort of stirring loneliness that she could not expect others to understand. Her companions were the placid water, the indistinct stars and a less familiar presence, the disease she pictured as an ocher stain spreading across her retinas, pulsating with arterial blood, no larger than a freckle but fully capable of exploding her life.

In August the decline in her vision seemed to pause, and as autumn slipped in she began to photograph the lake in a desultory way. By night, bringing the photos up on a computer screen in the complete darkness, in the stillness broken only by loons and killdeer, she studied the images without putting on the reading glasses that were now her constant companion. The pictures hovered before her not as photographs but as color fields, studies in the values of light, spectral abstractions. She watched them warily, like prey, and eventually they began to change under her unfocused gaze. After the long shapeless summer she felt her curiosity piqued—an idea forming—and by first snowfall she was back in New York, laying plans, studying books on the physics of light, filling notebooks with ideas in a large hand.

By the time she left for Cleveland she knew that her new art was to photograph not the things of the world, but the light that whispered through them.

She is traveling as lightly as a serious photographer can: a simple backpack for her clothes and books and computer, the battered aluminum hand-carry for her gear. By the time spring arrives she has lugged her bags through eleven airports, following her luminous itinerary through the pellucid light of the Caribbean, the smog of São Paulo, the prismatic display overhanging a cataract in the Paraguayan rainforest, the carbon-black light fused into the rocks of the Atacama Desert in Chile, where it has barely rained in hundreds of years. She has also been struck by a scooter that roared out of the blackness; cheated out of small change because she couldn't read the denominations of coins; tricked into hope, in Santiago, by a temporary rally of her vision. But she has kept going, and by the time she wanders at dawn through the cavernous modernity of the Houston airport she has shot fifteen thousand pictures. With a plane change she arrives in Denver, where she is greeted by her old AP colleague Peter Dawes.

Annie, he says, standing in a sunny nimbus behind the arrivals cordon. Over here, Annie.

She turns her head to target the familiar voice. The tunnel vision, severe now even in good light, forces her to pivot her head, owl-like, toward whatever she wants to see. Peter's wrinkled forehead enters her narrow lens first; she tracks downward to meet his blue eyes, which have not failed to note the effort it takes her to locate his waiting gaze. Any photographer knows the dance of composition, the sweep that frames a shot. For her, every glance is a composition now. It is a frightening burden, but it forces her to focus on what matters.

Peter's embrace is long and sincere. She has known him for thirty years, since Phnom Penh. In close-up his skin is a stained map: he has grown old.

How long? he asks as he steers the Land Rover across the high plains.

Since we've seen each other?

No. Until you can't see at all.

Anne considers this, the central question of her life.

Months. Or even weeks. There's no guarantee that I won't wake up blind tomorrow.

Dawes weighs this information and says: Then we'd better get to work right away.

They arrive at his mountain home in the late morning and the light is everything she has hoped for. This stop on her journey was carefully chosen. She plans to study the shots she's taken so far in the clear, unbiased mountain radiance, borrowing her friend's trusted eyes before moving on to shoot the raw radiation of the Utah desert. She'd plotted her odyssey so that the lowest-light stops came first, when her vision was at its compromised best; the brightest light is for last. Dawes leaves her bags in the guest room and begins downloading the work onto his computer. In the early days of her career it would have taken weeks of darkroom time to harvest it all, but now it flows quickly, effortlessly, the computer ingesting her photos with a burbling sound. They lunch on the sun-drenched stone patio, saying little, and by one o'clock are reviewing the Cleveland set in his studio.

They cull fifteen photos and run them through a spectroscopic analyzer, fingerprinting Lake Erie's friable light. Dawes tacks a print of each and its spectral graph to his cork wall, gathering evidence to test a hypothesis she cannot yet put into words—she has tried, but it still sounds too abstruse—and they move on to her sojourn on Anguilla, trading grey ice for azure. The spectra widen, unlimber themselves toward cerulean blue, the irregular hump of the curve shifting toward the ultraviolet. This light is more complex, says Dawes, and though his science doesn't ring quite true his perception seems dead on.

By late afternoon they are in the rainforest, but the natural light is failing and her sight is shutting down. It goes without saying that to continue by artificial light is out of the question. And so Dawes puts the computer to sleep and opens a bottle of Bordeaux and cooks her a fine steak. After dining on the patio, they move to deck chairs and lower them so that the whole sweep of the sky is overhead.

Can we see the Milky Way? she asks casually.

Yes, it's slightly toward your feet.

She cranes her head forward obediently, scanning the muddy heavens.

I can't even see the Milky Way, she says quietly. I will never see it again.

Dawes can't think of any comforting words to say, and so lets the silence speak for him. After some minutes he hears the sound of a stifled sob. She has been shot at in war zones, has nearly died in filthy backwater clinics, has lived a rootless and lonely existence for years, yet only now does he sense fear in her. At nine he puts her gently to bed, asking only harmless questions. Like Darra and all the friends she chooses, he is not one to demand explanations. Only as he is turning to go upstairs does she reach for his hand and squeeze it.

Do you want me to stay with you? he asks.

I know you're here, Peter, she replies after some thought. And I know you appreciate what I used to be able to do, the eye I had. That's more than enough.

Anne sleeps peacefully in the crisp mountain air and awakes ready to continue with the work. But over breakfast Dawes convinces her to take a short walk to a promontory where the light is, he says, extraordinary. They walk the gentle slope up his black-topped road and he takes her by the arm to divert her toward a granite outcrop overlooking the canyon. Her vision is worse today, periscopic: she scans the valley through her puny aperture, the land horizonless. In the shadows below, a long flank of evergreens is scarred with dead trees the color of a cicada husk. As best she can see, the light here is simple, obvious, of little interest. Dawes pivots her toward the east and she sees a sand-colored rill spotted with intrepid pines, hangers-on, the whole array washed in morning sun.

Do you see what I mean? asks Dawes quietly.

She does not. This light looks just as simple to her. She studies it as closely as she can, trusting his vision, but cannot see what he sees.

I don't see it, Peter, no.

The rock? The ochre, white, moss-green of it, with a charcoal undertone? Something massive about it? Look again, Annie.

Dawes, she says—and then, without warning, she is crying. She squeezes her eyes shut and leans into her old friend, her knees wavering.

Oh god, Peter, I can't see any of it. It's all flat. Underexposed. Dead.

Annie, he says, pulling her close. They have not held one another like this, hip to hip, since Phnom Penh, when they were in their thirties. She rests her chin on his shoulder for a few heartbeats and then pulls away, drying her eyes.

They walk back in silence, her field of vision contracted to a few feet, her steps unsteady. Dawes walks half a pace behind her, ready to take her arm if she should trip or lose her balance, though he is careful not to reveal this. The silence between them seems to rouse the birds, to awaken them in every tree. The smell of pine sap is strong in the heat. It would be a pleasant walk were it not for her condition. After a time she says: I'm like an accident victim who wakes up and realizes, only little by little, that she no longer has legs.

Somewhere in the midst of the afternoon's work—they are scanning the images from the Chilean desert now—she realizes that her sight is failing in real time, hour by hour. Something is changing quickly and for the worse.

In the year or so since her diagnosis she has harbored an imagined scene in her mind, one in which a woman awakes one morning to find that she has gone blind in the night; Anne has revisited the scene many times, wringing the fear out of it, until it has become nearly harmless. But a different scene is playing out on this sunny afternoon in Colorado. Now she is watching her sight drain away like water from a pool, swirling down into blackness, and it is the difference between dying in one's sleep and dying with full awareness of the event. She has never wanted to be awake for this final descent. Peter, she says suddenly, this isn't the right thing for me to be doing now. I'm sorry.

She pushes away from the work table and gets to her feet, disoriented.

Annie! What's going on?

I'm going blind now. Right now.

She looks frantically around the cluttered studio, scanning the wall with her prints and spectrograms, barely able to resolve the boundaries of things. The diameter of her visual field has shrunk to a few degrees, as if she is looking down the wrong end of a telescope. If there were an f/∞ she would be fast approaching it, clicking rapidly toward the negation of light, its complete denial.

She reaches for Dawes and says in a whisper, Peter, do you realize that yours is the last face this girl will ever see? She turns her dim eyes toward him, then touches his skin. After a time she says, Help me get to my bag.

They pick their way downstairs to her room. He stands beside her and supports her, sensing that she is losing ground to plain fear. Clumsily she digs through her road-worn backpack, throwing socks and panties and three pairs of readers onto the bed with abandon, frantic to find something . . . until, from a zipped inner pocket, she draws out a small brown bottle capped with an eyedropper. The label is stained with a viscous liquid and engraved with an ornamental script. She regards it for a moment as if she could read it, but it is he who reads the words *Tintura de Belladonna*.

Belladonna, Anne?

But she is still rummaging, coming up this time with a plastic bag that holds pressed white wildflowers half disintegrated into powder.

Anne, what is this?

Peter, I need you to help me out to the patio. To the sun. Right now.

He doesn't know what is happening, exactly, but he does as she says. Together they get her situated in one of the deck chairs and lower the back so that her face is inclined toward the sky like the sight of a sextant.

They are at altitude and the sun is scorching, flamelike on exposed skin; there is not a cloud in the sky. Let me get you a hat if you insist on being out here, Dawes says, and ducks back into the house. When he returns he sees the plastic bag with the dried flowers in her lap, empty now, then notices that she is chewing something. She swallows before he can speak. Annie, he demands, what did you just eat? What's going on here?

It is as if she's not heard him at all. Anne unscrews the top of the little brown bottle, draws an amber liquid into the dropper and carefully places three drops into each eye. An instant later she screams in pain, covering her face.

Damn it! she says, her eyes tearing profusely, her cheeks shining in the sun.

Annie! Talk to me! Dawes bends over her, squeezing her shoulder and giving her one brisk shake.

Rather than answer, she draws her hand back and exposes her eyes, opening them slowly. He sees that they are swollen and very dark, then realizes that her pupils are hugely dilated. He has never seen pupils so wide: they give her eyes a blank aspect, like the pupils of a cartoon character. But she is groaning softly now, making an animal sound, and on instinct he takes the hat he has brought and covers her face.

Peter, let me, she says, gently moving the hat away. Dawes realizes that she is staring directly into the sun.

Anne, no! What are you doing? You can't look straight into the sun!

It's not the sun anymore, she says, and then laughs at the notion, suddenly lighthearted.

What the hell are you talking about? Dawes places his body between her staring eyes and the dangerous star above.

Peter, in the name of our friendship, out of respect for me, move out of my light. Please, Peter. I know what I'm doing.

No, Anne, plainly you don't. No sane person . . .

Move! she commands him, and in her tone he hears the grit he has seen her exhibit countless times over the years, the mulish resolve. The Anne Sweigart he has always admired lies before him on his patio, close-dancing with her own blindness, and he knows he cannot outthink her. Dawes steps back, releasing the sun to drill down onto his dear friend. Good, she says simply. Thank you.

He watches her for what seems an eternity, her head turning a few degrees left or right from time to time as a chef might turn a filet to sear it evenly, small sounds of wonderment or pain escaping her as the sun scorches down. The light is so strong that the back of his neck is burning.

Anne, he says, his voice no louder than the burbling traffic of sparrows in the myrtle. Tell me what you see.

She smiles and says, I knew you would want to know.

With this she reaches for his big dry hand and takes it in hers for a moment, swinging it, squeezing it. He feels a lightness in her, an ease he can't account for. A jay caws, scattering the sparrows, and this makes her smile again.

I can hear everything now—everything. It's extraordinary. I can hear your heart beating, for example. Tok . . . tok . . . tok.

She is right: she keeps perfect time with the rapid throb in his chest.

But that's not what you asked, she says. You asked what I could see.

She considers for a moment and says: I see pure heat, Peter. I see the sound of birds. I see the color of this conversation. I see the scent of the pines. I see the edge of the sawgrass. I see you, Peter. I see you very clearly.

He looks at her eyes and they are wide open, the lids rolled back, the pupils matte black and very dry now. Anne regards the sun without pain, with no reflex to withdraw.

The light is all mine now, she says calmly.

With this she turns toward him and flashes an old smile, the smile he hasn't seen since the early days in Cambodia when they thought, briefly, that they might be in love. Dawes kneels beside her.

It's done, Anne says simply, and traces the contours of his face as if it is the map of a country she once knew but has long since forgotten.

One
Child
Policy

Go home, Uncle tells her with a poorly stifled yawn. It's getting bad out there.

He hardly need say it. For hours now she's been watching the snow roar down Eighth Avenue like a huge white horse on a frantic gallop. As she wipes down the tables by the window she can feel bitter cold seeping through the flimsy windows, invading the tiny restaurant in a stealthy, gradual assault. The mat inside the leaking door is stained with giant bootprints of slush that refuse to melt away.

The weather of America frightens her. In Chongqing she saw snow rarely—a tired grey dust drifting through the smog, not even settling to the ground—but she knows from television that

American snow can kill. As the night has worn on she's watched it mount on the window sills and has worried more and more about how she will get home when her shift is over. It seems as though the young black couple at the corner table will never leave; at ten o'clock they are still picking at their egg rolls and hot-sour soup, talking on and on in loud voices, their English nothing like the English she learned in school. She dreads visiting their table because she knows she will have to ask them to repeat whatever they say. She is also afraid they'll order something else and drag the night out even longer, making her trip home even more dangerous. To them the storm outside is romantic, the restaurant cozier for it, but to her it is an angry animal taller than a building. She feels it reaching into her body and squeezing her stomach with its cold hands. When Uncle finally tells her to go home she locks herself in the bathroom and vomits, the remains of her chow fun just an acid slurry in the toilet bowl.

It isn't only the weather that makes her worry about the trip home, though. It's also that her friend Chen has left early to meet his parents at Kennedy Airport and so cannot escort her back to Brooklyn. She's seen their picture: country people, the elderly father stooped and blind, the mother expressionless from a life of grinding work. Of course Chen must be there when they arrive. One can only imagine their disorientation as they enter the odd world that is New York after three days of travel. At these moments it is everything to have a loyal son.

Chen watches over his parents, but he watches over her too. He treats her as an elder brother would, smoking cigarettes in the alley once he's slid the last order of pan-fried noodles or shrimp toast onto her tray, killing time just so that she won't have to ride the dangerous trains and walk past the projects alone. She knows that after dropping her at her door, Chen has a forty-minute walk back to his place. He says he likes the walk, but she suspects he goes on foot because he can't afford to pay another subway fare, just as she can't afford to pay for an apartment closer to the train. The last thing a line cook wants to do after a ten-hour shift, after all, is spend more time on his feet, rushing down ill-lit streets after midnight. And so she is grateful to Chen in ways she cannot even begin to express. But tonight he's clocked out early, leaving Uncle to work the woks himself and her to find her way home alone. In the five months she's worked at the restaurant, it is the first time she's had to make the long trip without her protector by her side.

As she bends over the bathroom sink, rinsing the bile from her mouth, it occurs to her that she doesn't know exactly when her train stops running—another practical detail she's always entrusted to Chen. The first time they rode home together he explained that her train doesn't run all night, that at a certain hour it is necessary to change to a different line, but she never asked him what time it stops, and she has never worked this late. At the thought of it she feels she's going to faint. She grasps the edge of the sink but then gives in and falls to her knees, her forehead resting against the cold porcelain, her whole body heaving. What will happen if she can't get home? If she has to get off the train in some dangerous neighborhood she doesn't know, perhaps a neighborhood where they don't speak English at all, where she can't even ask for directions?

She has no friends other than Chen, not a single soul in the enormous city who can help her. As she kneels in the little bathroom her mind races and then freezes, as if the storm outside has reached into her thoughts and stopped them cold. But even so she knows that if she wants to get home at all, she must go now. Every minute that passes brings her closer to that unknown moment when her train will stop and she will be thrown out into the night the way some people in Chongqing abandon their unwanted baby girls in alleys and train yards. And so she gets to her feet, unlocks the door and walks carefully back into the dining room, trying to hide her panic.

Uncle cashes her out and sends her into the night with a frown. Be careful, he says in a scolding voice, as if she were doing something wrong by setting off on her own, and she wonders if he realizes that being careful is not enough. It was Uncle who taught her the basic rules of New York: never make eye contact; walk fast; don't stand near the edge of the train platform. But she now knows that these measures do not stop bad things from happening. Uncle was wrong about another thing, too. Stay away from the blacks, he told her—yet it was a white man, a customer with a yellowing beard that stank of cigarettes, who had waited for the end of her shift and jerked her into his car and hurt her.

And so she doesn't trust Uncle's advice. She can no longer

call him Uncle to his face, either; he isn't a real uncle, but some more distant relative from Chengdu who happened to appear in Chongqing a few months after her mother's death. She remembers the meal her father's new girlfriend laid out for this near-stranger, how the talk turned to America and his golden life there, the thousand questions her father asked him about New York, and then her father's announcement, at the end of a long evening floating on a sea of beer, that he would send her to America to work in Uncle's restaurant.

Her father didn't even look at her, much less ask her what she thought of the idea, and she is certain she knows why: she was only an obstacle to him, now that her mother was gone. He ignored her, bullied by his pushy girlfriend and her plans to marry him, which everyone knew were just plans to marry his money. Why else would a pretty young widow want to marry this man whose looks had been ruined by too many cigarettes and too much beer? The sorry truth was that whatever money he'd had from his plumbing supply shop was long gone. How long would it be before the new Mrs. Xiao realized it?

Some months later, sitting at a table in America on a slow night in Uncle's restaurant, Chen had listened to her story, watched how she told it without giving in to tears, and asked the one question that changed her opinion of her father forever. Do you think, he asked, that your father's girlfriend wants to have a child with your father?

How would I know? she'd answered. He's so old! What does it matter?

Because, Chen said delicately, you were his one child.

Yes? she'd said, not understanding why he was stating this plain fact.

Chen had paused gently, seeing that she still didn't understand, and then said:

You were the one child permitted.

In that instant the truth turned in her like a tumbler in a lock. She was speechless. Of course, she realized: if the new Mrs. Xiao wanted a child, her father's first child would have to be subtracted from the equation. That was the law, the cold-hearted math. One family, one child. The fine was steep and unforgiving; the heartless policy lived on.

Perhaps her father would even have to prove that she had died. As the implications of it unfolded in her mind she could clearly picture her father in one of the windowless cubbies, in the slums, where illegal business was transacted—perhaps the same place where he'd bought her illegal travel papers. Now he would be buying her faked death certificate so that the new Mrs. Xiao could bear his child without risk of the enormous fine. It seemed undeniable to her as she ruminated on it.

For three nights in a row she lay on the dirty floor of her basement apartment crying at the thought of his betrayal. Perhaps in Chongqing she was already dead, erased from the rolls of the living to clear the way for some infant brother or sister she would never know. What would her father have done if she still lived there? Would he have had her poisoned, shot, kidnapped? Killed her with his own hands so that he could marry his arrogant girlfriend and get her pregnant just to prove that he still could? Her mother's poor ghost must be weeping, wherever it was. She wished it were here in her apartment, close to her, comforting her with its soft hands. But it seemed that not even the ghosts had followed her to New York.

The door of Uncle's restaurant slams behind her and she turns into the driving snow, starting up Eighth Avenue toward the subway. The street is oddly quiet, the sounds of taxis and buses muffled by the heavy blanket of white. But the wind comes in broad slapping gusts. By the time she reaches the first intersection she is already shivering, the frozen sidewalk pushing through her flimsy sneakers and snaking up the bones of her legs. Her threadbare mittens are useless against the cold; her cotton jacket is meant for a fall day, not a winter night. Today is her eighteenth birthday and this is her gift: to be thrown into the frozen and dangerous American night, entirely alone.

As she waits for the light to turn she feels she might not make it all the way to her apartment. The nausea has made her weak; the cold is relentless, and she has walked only a little way. Tears freeze at the corners of her eyes, binding her lashes to her face. Her cheeks ache in the frigid air. But then the light changes and her legs set her in motion as if under the control of someone else. The sensation reminds her of riding sidesaddle behind her father on his bicycle when she was a girl, of being carried along for a ride. Her legs carry her like the legs of another, alternating between numbness and flaring pain inside the flimsy polyester pants Uncle makes her wear. She is wearing leggings under the pants—a trick Chen taught her—but they do little to stop the cold.

She passes almost no one on the street. The restaurants are closed now and the weather is keeping people inside. She is afraid that the cold might kill her, that the wind might knock her to the ground, that a stranger in a car might offer her refuge and she might accept it. She bows her head and keeps walking, measuring each step like an acrobat on a tightrope.

No one, not even her friend Chen, knows that it is her birthday. Her father would be the last to remember it; Uncle would neither know nor care. While her mother was alive she was never lonely—they spent hours together, holding hands like sisters—but now she is lonelier than a widow after the funeral guests go home, lonelier than a river locked under ice. It occurs to her that her loneliness will now go everywhere she goes: she is lonely in New York now, but she would be lonely back in Chongqing too. Her loneliness is her midnight shadow.

There is no one on the sidewalk but her. She can't remember a time when this was true. In New York as in Chongqing one is surrounded by people, by their voices and demands and body odors. There is safety in the crowd as long as you keep your money close. Yet now there is no one but her. As she approaches the next intersection she steals a glance over her shoulder to make sure she isn't being followed. There is no one walking behind her, but a black car trundles over the snow-packed street, matching her pace.

At the corner she looks down Thirty-Second and is relieved to see a police cruiser idling in a billow of exhaust. She crosses the street to be nearer to it and sees a Korean-looking policeman dozing behind the wheel, his mouth agape. Even a sleeping policeman is better than no policeman at all, and she lingers near the cruiser until the black car pulls through the intersection and disappears into the blizzard. When she's sure it is gone she continues on her way, skirting patches of ice that have formed near manhole covers and other sources of warmth, her smooth sneakers unsure on the changeable ground.

She is walking as carefully as she can, but still it happens. Half a block from the subway stairs she steps on hidden ice and her foot slides suddenly out from under her, and she is on the frozen sidewalk at midnight in a hard city she doesn't understand. She sits in the snow and cries to herself until she hears her mother's voice tell her to get to her feet and go home. And so she picks herself up and makes her way to the subway, feeling her mother's invisible hand at the small of her back, her intimate voice in her ear.

———————

Chen said something strange once, just a passing remark as she told him about her mother one night. It was the first anniversary of her mother's death; as the day approached she'd felt her mother's ghost hovering nearby, an elusive presence, there and not there. She awoke that morning to the scent of the ghost's lilac soap; then as she dressed she thought she heard it speak near the door. She ran over and touched the knob delicately, the way one might touch a chrysalis, listening carefully, but the voice was gone. Her mother had been dead a year now, but in a way she had not yet died.

As she and Chen walked to the train that night she'd started telling him the terrible story of her mother's last day. She couldn't recall now how the topic had come up, but in the space of a few blocks the whole sad tale tumbled out of her—the way her mother left before dawn for the clinic, not telling anyone why; the way her father refused to go see her; the way the nurses wouldn't let her see her mother when she went alone to the hospital. Two of them had been stern and cruel, but another had taken her behind a curtained wall and there her mother lay, curled up like an inchworm, a tube in her nose, her face a mask. Ma! she'd whispered, but the nurse pinned her arms so that she couldn't throw them around her mother. She can't hear you, the nurse said in a matter-of-fact tone, and as she tried to make sense of these words she saw a red stain growing on the sheet near her mother's hips. She watched in panic as the nurse called for help and threw the sheet back to reveal a stream of dark blood flowing from between her mother's legs. Her mother groaned, a noise she'd never heard her make, but though she seemed to be in pain her dazed expression didn't change at all. All at once the room was full of people. *Get out!* someone snapped, but in the confusion of the moment no one noticed that she stayed, hovering in the corner of the room, trying to grasp what was happening. The red flow from between her mother's legs was unstoppable now. She felt the nurses' panic and heard an alarm go off, a machine complaining that her mother was in trouble, and the alarm spoke for her because her voice was locked in her throat.

A doctor never came, she'd told Chen as the story spilled from her a year later. *My mother was dying in front of me and a doctor never even came.*

Chen had walked on, slowing his stride a little. And then he'd said something that didn't make sense to her at the time:

They don't care if women in that position die, do they? Minus two is worth more than minus one. They know they're being watched. The cadres are counting up lives all the time.

She'd wanted to ask Chen what he meant but there was something in his tone that made her hold her tongue. And so she'd let it go.

———————

The train comes right away, and she is surprised to see it so full of people at nearly midnight. There is a seat open next to a muscular white man with a shaved head, but the green flame tattooed across his scalp and the ox-ring in his nose frighten her, and she prefers to stand. He looks like a thief or a murderer; something virulent and wild is running loose in his hard gaze. There is no one in all of Chongqing as frightening as the people she sees on the subway every night. She is still shocked at how many of them smell like urine.

She sways with the train as it trundles through stop after stop, clutching the silver pole and fighting sleep. She is as tired as she was after the journey over from China. Eventually the train passes under the river, and she holds her breath as she always does, but tonight Chen is not here to tease her about it. She imagines him at Kennedy Airport, waiting outside the immigration barrier, searching the crowd of Chinese faces for the two that he knows.

At Atlantic Avenue she spills onto the platform with a dozen other riders and is waiting to transfer to her train when she realizes that the man with the tattooed head is standing right beside her. He is staring at her openly, looking her up and down, and she doesn't need to look at him to sense his disgust. He hates her—why? As the train roars out of the tunnel he says something in a threatening tone, but with the screech of the wheels she can't understand his English. The impossible noise envelops them as if a blanket has been thrown over their heads, shutting him in with her.

She counts the doors as the train slows, trying to judge where to stand so that she can race into the car first and move toward the back, away from him. But when the doors hiss open she is midway between two entries. She waits to see what the tattooed man will do, which door he will pick—she waits until she can feel the doors about to slam shut—but the man waits too, as if daring her to move first. When the metallic announcement begins she darts toward the door to her right, escaping into the car just as the door closes.

There is no one behind her. She feels her throat tightening and makes her way down the aisle as the train jerks out of the station. At last she sits down next to a kindly looking black woman dressed all in purple, her big arms folded over her breasts as if gathering in children. The woman smiles sadly at her and then looks out the scratched window into the weird gloom of the tunnel.

It isn't long before she realizes that something is wrong. She is lost in thoughts of her mother, her heart soft and unsteady in her chest, when she notices the Bergen Street platform go speeding past. Her train always stops at Bergen; she knows the station because there is an old Chinese man who sits on a crate playing the erhu for tips, lending her and Chen thirty seconds of peace while the doors are open. But tonight the train hammers right past Bergen. She stands in her seat and cranes forward to look at the route map, and realizes in an instant that she's on the wrong train: her train is the red line; this one is green. It must be obvious that she's panicking, because the woman next to her pulls on her coat, gently guiding her back into her seat.

Caught the wrong train? she asks. Where you going?

New Lots.

The woman laughs as if she's told a joke. "New Rots," huh?

Lots, she says, enunciating as clearly as she can. This sound is hard for her.

Please, where I go?

New Lots? says the woman, looking at her watch. You got to think about the midnight service. You got to consider that.

Then the woman starts talking faster, in that accent that is so hard to follow, and all at once she's on her feet, squeezing past as the train slows. The woman is going to leave her. But then she turns and says something. It is just a jumble of foreign words that don't add up.

Say again? Please?

The woman repeats what she's said in exactly the same way. The only part of it that makes sense is "Crown Heights."

Crown Heights! This is the name of a stop; she's heard it announced a hundred times.

Get off Crown Heights? she asks. But the brakes are screeching and the woman doesn't hear her.

Crown Heights, she repeats to herself. This must be where she changes to the red train. There is a map of the subway system near the door and she can see that, yes, she can transfer from green to red at Crown Heights. A wave of relief comes over her: it will be all right after all. Even without Chen she will find her way home.

——————

At the Crown Heights stop she is the first out of her car, and no sooner does her sneaker touch the platform than she sees a red train trundling out of the dark tunnel. Everything is going perfectly now. She crosses the platform as if she has all the time in the world, suddenly at ease. Even the prospect of walking the eight blocks from the final stop to her apartment doesn't worry her now. As the train slows it occurs to her that her mother must be watching over her, guiding her steps, keeping her from harm. This is what a mother does, even from beyond death. Perhaps the dead know things they could not have known in life: the particulars of the New York subway system, for example. Perhaps the dead never stop learning.

The train stops and its doors slide open. With a single step she is on board and she easily finds a seat toward the front of the car. A harsh announcement comes over the speaker and she doesn't bother to decode it. She is on her way home now. The train lugs itself into motion and she slumps down in her seat, letting herself breathe fully for the first time in hours. Two stops go by quickly, the train pulling itself up from the tunnel into the night along the way, mounting a trestle in the tireless snow.

As the train picks up speed the connecting door between her car and the next jerks open. Her body jerks in response, for she's fallen asleep, lulled by the train's rocking. She is fully awake in an instant. When she opens her eyes she sees the man with the flamed tattoo on his scalp bursting through the connecting door.

As he struts down the aisle the man slaps the seat backs with his big hands; she notices that his forearms are tattooed with a symbol that looks like twin lightning bolts, or perhaps an angular SS. He is walking directly toward her but has not yet noticed her. As he passes an elderly black man he rips the orange hat from his head and throws it to the floor with a humorless laugh, then shouts something in the old man's ear. The man only shrinks in his seat, not protesting.

She shrinks too, pretending to sleep. But then she hears the huge man pause a few feet away from her and suddenly there is a crashing kick to her ribs, a violent blow that throws her onto the shuddering floor of the car. She is too stunned to feel the pain of the boot until it kicks her a second and a third time. On reflex she curls up in self-defense the way her mother curled up on her deathbed, and when she dares to open her eyes she sees a smear of her own blood against the hard plastic seat. The boot is against her ear now, pressing her face to the rubber floor mat, its pressure increasing until she thinks it will crush her head like a melon. But then it is gone, and a moment later she feels the sharp toe probing into the cleft between her legs, prodding at her the way it might prod at a dead thing washed up on a beach.

With a sharp jab between her legs the tattooed man forces her to roll over. He towers over her, roaring in a voice that doesn't sound human. She sees now that there is something wrong with one of his eyes and the brow above it, some violent rearrangement of parts that looks barely survivable. He pauses for a moment, examining her, then spits out a word she doesn't know: Gook! Gook! he yells, kicking her with each repetition. And now the pain comes fast and hard. It shoots between her ribs like an electric eel, darting up through her small body until she screams. She rolls onto her belly to protect herself, but it is no use. She is completely at his mercy.

The beating subsides again and when she takes a stealthy breath she hears the man above her laughing as if someone has told a clever joke. There is a smell of urine; she feels a warm stream touch her neck and slide down her nape, saturating her collar with a dank stink. When she opens her eyes in alarm it is to the sight of frayed black jeans and the silver tip of a huge boot. Fucking gook, he says again, and this time the stream is aimed at her face. His work done, the tattooed man walks casually down the length of the car and slumps into a bench seat near the far door, sighing loudly like a man who has just done a hard bit of work.

<hr />

She prays that he will get off at the next stop, that he will leave her to unfold her arms and legs and see what is broken and what is whole. But the doors open and close and he is still in the car with her.

Now, though, someone else catches his attention: two loud boys with cheap gold chains, dark glasses and baggy pants burst onto the train and sit down opposite the tattooed man. One is taunting and slapping at the other, head cocked back in challenge, and they don't even notice the small woman crumpled at the far end of the car. She watches the boys secretly as the tattooed man watches them, feeling something build in him although he hasn't moved a muscle since they boarded. She sees too the moment when they notice him, and she feels their fear—these rough boys on a late-night train who on any other night would terrify her. The train is closing in on its next stop, above ground now, when with stupid bravado one of the boys raps the other on the knee and says, Look at that bad motherfucker. Thinks he's fuckin' Hitler, the motherfucker.

This is all it takes. The tattooed man is on them in an instant. As the train screeches into the station she sees the flash of a knife and then a great arc of blood whirling through the air next to the boy's head, and she is somehow on her feet and then somehow out on the platform in the frigid air, cast out into the unknown wilds of Brooklyn as the train pulls away and leaves her completely alone.

She finds her way to a bench under a stern electric light and sits to compose herself. She needs to inventory the damage and work out what to do next.

Her ribs are shouting with pain and it hurts to breathe. Gingerly she tests her limits, inhaling a little more with each breath until the swell of her chest makes the pain unbearable. It is as she does this that she realizes she is not afraid. Perhaps she has reached the outer limit of her fear; or perhaps her mother's ghost is soothing her with its invisible hands, hovering behind her in the frozen night. Whatever the case, she feels very calm now. In time she stands and washes the urine from her face with snow, then looks at the route map under the light, methodically tracing out the night's journey until she locates the station name that appears on the sign above her head.

She knows that she cannot get on the train again. She will walk home from wherever she is. But the map shows no street names, no neighborhood names, nothing that would help her know whether she is five blocks or five miles from her building, or how to find her way through the dark, snowy streets to reach it.

There is only one real option. Walking carefully down the icy steps, her right leg and side aching sharply, she descends to the street and begins to walk under the elevated trestle, knowing that eventually it will lead her home.

She walks for more than an hour, passing gutted cars and boarded-up pawn shops and buildings scrawled with tirades of graffiti, seeing barely a soul on the deserted streets. At one point she must trudge up a steep embankment and pick her way across a no man's land of tracks from another line that cross under the trestle, terrified that she will lose her footing as a train flies past. Buses trundle blindly through the intersections, glowing bubbles of life that go about their business like deep-sea creatures, oblivious to her presence.

The street is deeply drifted with snow for blocks at a time; her sneakers and thin black pants are caked in ice, her exhausted legs numb from trudging through it. Still the snow is spilling down in great slow torrents of white. As she picks her way through the night, fitful trains pass overhead and shower orange sparks down upon her as if it is New Year's on the Jialing. They pock the drifts around her, and when a few touch her cheek she does not regret the momentary prick of heat.

She has fallen countless times now, unable to keep her footing in the slick sneakers, and as she makes her way through a deserted intersection she falls yet again, landing hard in the frozen street. Fist-sized clots of snow have made their way into her clothes, but she has long since given up trying to remove them. She gets to her hands and knees in the middle of the road, numb with fatigue, fighting the temptation to lie down and sleep just where she is. But when she looks up she sees a familiar set of stairs coming down from the elevated trestle, a familiar purple sign for a hair salon, the yellow awning of a liquor store she recognizes—and realizes with sudden relief that she has reached her stop at last. In her exhaustion she had not even noticed that she was nearing it, coming into known territory, but now here it is, the platform rising up in the bronze glare of the streetlights like the gantry of a rocket or a gallows of battered steel. She is nearly home.

By the time she reaches her apartment it is past three and the radiator has long since clanked off into silence. When she locks the door behind her and sighs with exhaustion, her breath pirouettes quickly in the half-light, a little soul dancing away. And now she starts to shiver. Perhaps it was anxiety that kept her body from this natural reflex during the endless walk home, but now it comes over her like a seizure, rattling her limbs with terrible force, and she hurries to the bathroom and turns the shower on full strength. She waits for the hot water to come and climbs over the lip of the tub without even taking her clothes off.

At first the warmth is an indescribable relief. She sobs as its fingers reach through her frozen clothes and touch her stiff limbs. But after a few moments, as blood begins to rush back toward her numb skin, a fiery pain moves quickly over her body as if she's been doused in gasoline and set aflame. In panic she shuts the shower off and begins to tear at her clothes, finally standing naked under the bare electric bulb.

She examines her body in the cracked mirror. It is her eighteenth birthday—she is officially an adult now—but her skin is flushed like a baby's cheek, blotched with crimson. There is a long tongue of virulent red that crosses between her small breasts and rides down to her rounded belly: this must have been where the snow breached the zipper of her jacket, passed through her shirt and spread itself against her skin. Even her cropped black hair, pasted lifelessly against one broad cheek like a leaf rotting at the bottom of a gutter, seems to have suffered.

All this is troubling, but then she turns slightly and discovers the enormous, yellow-black bruises along her side, the wounds left by the tattooed man's steel-toed boot. The skin was jaggedly broken at the soft cleft below her ribs, the whole area just a dark scab now. She touches the dried blood carefully, recoiling at the pain. It is as if she's been hit by a speeding car. At the sight of her own battered body she feels the nausea rising again in a sudden geyser and all at once she is vomiting, spattering the mirror with bile. When it is over she struggles for breath and then cries out at the pain in her ribs, in her skin, in the marrow of her bones. She has never felt so alone.

A few minutes later she wraps herself in a blanket and lies down on the floor at the exact center of the basement apartment's single room. The linoleum is cold but she needs to feel the stability of the earth beneath her. The floor cradles her as the hand of a mother cradles the head of her newborn child.

In the deep of the night she closes her eyes and thinks of her own mother, of the blood she spilled on the last day of her life, and silently asks her mother's ghost to come to her, to filter through the painted cinderblock wall and lie down beside her one child and explain what has happened. She imagines her mother's lilac scent, her teasing voice, the softness of her small hands—imagines these things in great and loving detail. After a long while she hears her mother's voice in the room and opens her eyes with joy, scanning the darkness for the presence she has often felt but never seen, but there is nothing. She feels that her mother is close . . . why does she always hide herself?

Her eyes drift to the small windows near the low ceiling which look out onto the sidewalk, at boot level, and the irregular pinwheels of snow make her think of her mother's cremation ashes spinning up into the heavy air of Chongqing. Her father had dropped the urn, fumbled it in the narrow street only moments after it came into his hands, and nothing about her mother's death seems quite as sad as that careless moment. Now she needs the snow to cease, to stop reminding her of things she should forget, but the snow doesn't care about her. As she closes her eyes and tries to quiet her throbbing body she surrenders to sleep at last, the long day's fight over, the night almost gone.

She dreams of a wedding feast. There is a long table laden with gabbling guests, a Western-style sugar cake, the neighbors from the building drunk and voluble. Uncle is there in his stained chef's tunic, too, although now a tattoo of green flames spreads its fingers across his bald pate. A chill runs through her at the sight of him, as if everything that has made her suspect Uncle's motives is now confirmed once and for all.

As she scans the wedding party, her dreaming self feels that it would like to leave, but then her gaze falls upon the guests of honor. At the center of the banquet table sit Chen and herself, holding hands like American teenagers. Chen is wearing his black-and-white checked cook's pants, she her waitress uniform, but her hair is woven with scarlet ribbons and her eyes are made up like the supermodel Liu Wen's. She is a beautiful bride: this her sleeping self sees clearly.

In her dream there is nothing strange in marrying Chen. It seems like something she has expected for a very long time, perhaps since childhood, though in waking life she has known him for less than a year. He is tall and broad-faced, with deep, stately eye folds like a Mongol nomad, and his shy smile is charming. She watches him chat amiably with his new mother-in-law—for her late mother is there at his elbow, alive and happy, and it is wonderful to see her laugh and shine with joy. Chen's blind old father and careworn mother look on, too, eclipsed by their new inlaws, by this bright spirit come to life, but they too seem happy in their way. Her own father is nowhere to be seen.

It seems to be summer in the dream, but a light snow begins to fall on the wedding party nonetheless, and it is the bride herself who stands to announce that the time has come for the newlyweds to taste a traditional fertility dish. From somewhere she produces an ornate blue platter heaped with noodles that are actually— she proudly declares—the fallopian tubes of a dozen sows. In the dream they are alive, swarming hungrily on the plate, but the bride is neither alarmed nor disgusted; she is happy. As she plucks the first of them up with enameled chopsticks and swallows it whole she is no longer separate from the dreamer watching her. Together they feel the wriggling thing run loose in her body and find its way to her belly, her womb.

A moment later she hears a high squeal of laughter from behind her, and then another from in front, and another from above. Her world is brimming with invisible children now, a whole reckless tribe of them—not the one child permitted her dear mother but a dozen boys and girls, a sprawling, noisy family she has made with Chen. She cannot see their faces, nor can she see Chen or her mother or any of the wedding guests now. But the children's voices carry her aloft like a May wind lifting her exhausted body from below. When the sun finally wakes her there is a long moment when she could be anywhere, in any country or millennium, moving through the world of ten thousand things with all the fleet joy of a ghost. Her body is lying very still, but her mind's eye is on the move, untrammeled, lighter than smoke.

In time she becomes aware of a hand nestled within hers like a tame bird, a sensation so familiar that at first she thinks nothing of it. She squeezes it gently, taking its measure, and is not surprised when it braids its delicate fingers into hers.

Ma! she says in the sun-filled stillness of her apartment, and turns her head to see where the endless night has taken her.

The
Release

Helen spent almost all her evenings with him, just as she had through all the twenty-two years of their married life. After loading the dishwasher and buffing the granite countertop to a pleasing shine she would change into her mauve pajamas, or in summer a nightgown she'd embroidered with tiny tea roses, and slip into the den, knotting a bathrobe loosely around her waist. Denny would be waiting for her there after his obligatory cigarette on the back steps, calmly taking in the mood of the evening, a great stillness surrounding him. Perhaps he was thinking, perhaps not; she could never tell. Often he seemed to be listening for something, as if expecting a faint knock at the door.

She didn't know what was in his mind and it seemed somehow rude to ask.

The old house had grown quieter and quieter since the children had moved out. She and Denny spurned television, and the Thomases on the other side of the garden wall were elderly and reclusive. And so a kind of solitude had set in. Denny seemed to find great solace in it, and Helen would do anything to defend whatever gave him solace; he deserved no less after decades of relentless work. She would pad in behind him and take her place at the end of the couch, settling in comfortably amid its coppery fleurs-de-lis and waiting for him to break the silence. But there was no guarantee that he would, and eventually she would take up her book club novel and read the evening away, under the gun to finish it before the next meeting.

As she read she never lost awareness of Denny in the closeness of the room, nor of the sound of summer crickets, nor of the hush of December snowfall in the yard outside. Her attention was honed to a fine edge now, as precise as the steel drafting pens and Bézier curves his grandfather had left him when he was still a boy. Though there were evenings when they did not exchange a single word between dinner and their goodnights, she'd never felt so close to her husband, and even told her sister June she felt her life was fuller for the quiet that filled the house. It did not separate her from Denny, but connected her to him, as though the silence were the water of an ocean they shared.

—————

Little of this had changed with his death, except that now she dined alone before moving to the den. Denny still waited for her there, gathered into himself; she still read away the evenings, aware of him in every moment. At ten o'clock she would turn off the reading lamp, straighten the throw pillows and say goodnight to him before heading upstairs. There was a new kind of pang at this moment, of course, a sadness so deep she still couldn't confess it to others: as she stood before his urn she felt like a woman poised at the edge of a cavern of unknown depth, a cavern that wanted to swallow her alive. Sometimes she would speak to him. *Good night,* she might say simply, or, once, *I miss you so much.*

On other nights she would take a chamois from the drawer—carefully, as if the tiny movement might disturb his concentration—and gently shine the green porcelain, straightening the urn before she climbed the stairs to bed.

The truth was that she had no idea what to do with his ashes, with this pot of dust that was somehow Denny.

I have to do the *right* thing, Helen told her sister as they picked over limp salads at the mall. But no one tells you what that is.

They have those little vaults you can lease, said June in a low voice, framing an invisible compartment with her hands. You know, in cemeteries.

No, that's horrible. He wouldn't want to be around all those dead people.

The irony of this statement lay on the table before them for a long moment before they caught each other's eye. June attempted a smile; Helen looked away.

Now you see how hard it is to make sense of, Helen said with unintended sharpness. I don't know how to think about where he is now. Or *what* he is.

It's quite an adjustment. I can only imagine.

It's good that Paul takes such good care of himself. I hope you never lose him.

This was a sore point between them, though neither would admit it. While it could fairly be said that Denny had smoked and worked himself into an early death, June's husband was a model of healthy aging, jogging around their gated community at dawn, meditating, heaping his plate with fruit and vegetables. *He'll outlive me by a thousand years,* June was fond of saying. *He'll be out there with his fishing pole when the glaciers melt, casting for Alaska salmon.* But since Denny's stroke and the heart attack that had fatally followed it, June no longer said these things to her older sister. She pushed the remains of her salad aside.

How important is it that you and the kids be able to . . . visit him? she asked gently.

I wish I knew. I don't like trapping him in a jar just to suit that need.

What about—

Scattering his ashes?

You could find a really lovely place, Helen, a place that meant a lot to him.

Helen sighed, exhausted. She looked out into the mall, into the swarm of strangers, and it was the older women who attracted her gaze. How many of them had been through what she was going through? Could she guess which were widows and simply ask for advice?

June watched her sister carefully, plaiting her paper napkin like an origami crane. When it seemed Helen would never look at her again she put the napkin aside and leaned forward.

Have you asked the kids what they think? she said, and held her breath.

At first Helen seemed not to have heard. Her tired eyes continued sizing up a trio of elderly women who were resting on a banquette outside Nordstrom. But then her back stiffened and she confronted her sister with a stare.

Ask the kids? Are you serious?

They might have opinions.

It's none of their business.

Helen! Denny was their father. Of course it's their business.

That's not what I mean. They're too young to know anything about death. They still think they're immortal.

Maybe helping you decide this would help them grow through that.

Do you think Brett would have good advice on what to do with his father's ashes when he can't even be bothered to look for a real job? And Brittany—she's on bed rest! I can't bother her with this.

You shouldn't just dismiss them.

And you shouldn't lecture me on how to parent.

With this Helen stood, laid a twenty-dollar bill on the table and began to walk away as if her companion had left an hour before her.

Jesus, Helen, I'm sorry, all right? June said, falling in beside her sister as she tacked toward the mall entrance. The revolving doors spun like turbines in a waterworks, exchanging one bundle of flotsam for the next. As they neared the car Helen abruptly stopped.

And what about *Sonoma?* she demanded. I suppose you think she'd have good advice too?

June found herself offended by these words—offended on behalf of her benign, childlike niece with the romantic name. After all these years Helen could not say her step-daughter's name without a trace of scorn at the absurdity of it, or perhaps at the way it invoked a time in Denny's life when he lived for pleasures Helen could not comprehend. But in the end it was only a name, and Sonoma was a difficult, irascible forty-year-old woman with the mental age of a first-grader, a woman capable of sudden clinging affection and also, in the next moment, screaming anger. She was mercurial but also oddly consistent, because her mind was frozen in time: she had barely changed as Denny ended his first marriage, took on the challenge of caring for her as a single parent, launched his career, courted Helen, fathered a second round of children and finally made the agonizing decision, with his practically minded second wife, to place Sonoma in institutional care. Through it all Sonoma had been constant, devoted to anyone who showed her kindness. She did not deserve Helen's scorn.

Don't bring Sonoma into this, Helen, said June.

Helen thought for a long mile, hitting all the stoplights wrong, and finally said, You're right, June. That was uncalled for.

After a time June asked: Does Maya know that Denny's gone?

At the mention of Denny's first wife, Helen's color rose: June saw it in the waning light, sorry she'd asked the question. But it was a fair question. After all these years, after raising a family with Denny and finally cradling his head as he died, her sister was still bitter toward a woman who had already passed out of Denny's life when Bobby Kennedy was killed.

I wouldn't know, Helen replied. I mailed her the notice but never heard a word back. Typical.

Try again, said June calmly. I know you hate her but she needs to know. And don't be afraid to ask the kids what to do about Denny. Maybe they can help. It will be good for all of you.

Helen pulled up beside June's house, her gaze veiled. They said their goodbyes like strangers who had shared a brief train ride, talking of nothing important, the passing landscape more interesting than the fitful conversation.

That evening Helen thought of nothing but her children, wondering what they could possibly know of death.

Each of them had worried her to distraction at times. As a girl of twelve Brittany had been a precocious tease; she was the first in her class to develop womanly curves, the first to sprout breasts, very possibly the first to let a boy touch her. They worried then about her spaghetti-strap tank tops, about the prominent nipples—Helen's—that no bra could quite conceal. They worried that she would get herself pregnant and abort the baby in some horrible way, or marry the useless teen father and wreck her life before it really began. And so it would be some years before they understood that the real threat to their daughter was not sex, but food. Looking at the girl of twelve, who could have imagined her now, obese in her frilly king-sized bed, her first pregnancy gravely threatened by an addiction to Dr Pepper and canned onion rings and Kit Kat bars—poisons which her ignorant husband continued to procure for her?

As Helen washed her supper dishes it suddenly struck her that she was certain Brittany would lose the child. She had not doubted it for a moment. *Horrible,* she said aloud at the sink, but did not know whether the word described the coming miscarriage or herself.

It was like this now: blunt thoughts she'd never have allowed herself while Denny was alive now flowed freely through her mind. Sometimes they escaped the confines of her imagination and went crashing into the world. She'd been shocked more than once by the things that leapt from her own mouth lately.

Only a week before, for example, as she walked home from an awkward coffee with Win Stewart, Denny's former partner, she turned a corner to find her twenty-two-year-old son squatting on a skateboard in the sidewalk as if he were only ten. The image struck her sweetly at first: she melted a little at the memory of her shy boy sitting exactly like this on a Saturday afternoon, his Giants cap turned backward as he chatted with Robbie Smits or

Justin Trimble, his jeans scuffed with grass. She had loved that little boy to death. In an instant, though, her heart closed. The Brett before her now still wore a backward baseball cap over his bleached hair, but this one said METALLICA in stark letters. This Brett wore Ray-Bans he could ill afford, and spoke into a tiny microphone on a cord that dangled from a cell phone, rocking the skateboard back and forth with a rhythm that struck his mother as lascivious. A boy with a skateboard and a grown man with a skateboard are, after all, entirely different creatures.

Brett, she said, standing over him as he continued to talk on the phone. The Ray-Bans inclined slightly upward, unreadable, as his long fingers brought the tiny microphone closer to his mouth. She thought he might swallow it. She might as well have been talking to a praying mantis.

Brett, she said again, nudging him with the toe of her red flat. Grudgingly he ended his call and shambled to his feet. He was a head taller than her but slumped so much that they were eye to eye—or would be, if she could see his eyes.

Take off those sunglasses, said Helen tartly. Right now.

The sun hurts my eyes.

Why should it? That's not normal. You embarrass yourself wearing sunglasses like those.

Is this really about me, Mom? I don't think so.

Do you know what, Brett? You're right. It's not about you at all. It's about how hard I find it to like you lately.

At this she turned on her heel and began to walk away, head high but heart collapsing with anguish. What had she said? She fought the urge to run back to him, to say how sorry she was, to gather her man-child in her arms. None of this would help, she knew, so she kept walking away, careful not to rush. The moment she entered the house she disintegrated into tears, disgusted with herself, as ashamed as a child caught in a hurtful lie.

But it was worse than a lie. It was the truth. She had told him exactly how she felt.

She was sitting on the hallway floor with her knees drawn up when her cell phone buzzed with a text message. Thinking it was Brett, she scrambled to fetch it from her blazer, desperate to apologize, but the message was from Win Stewart. *Thanks for today,* it said. *Dinner Chez Panisse soon?*

It was more than she could bear, this confusing attention from Denny's partner of thirty years. What had begun as kindhearted concern in the wake of Denny's death now seemed to be careening toward something else entirely. The thought made her frantic precisely because she could so easily picture herself taking up with him. She knew so much of his world—it was Denny's—and he had taken on a graceful humility since losing his wife to ovarian cancer. But what would Denny think? She couldn't shake the feeling that her late husband was watching them in alarm as they sipped coffee or reminisced or strolled the de Young, letting the thing ripen gradually between them.

She decided to let the text go, setting the phone on the hard parquet and spinning it idly. Win would be left to wonder. Would he still find her attractive if he knew how she'd treated her son minutes after leaving him?

That evening she found it impossible to sit in the den and instead took her book up to the rocker by the bedroom window, the air of censure thick in the house. She couldn't concentrate on the novel in her hands. By nine she had abandoned it, brushed her teeth, taken her blood pressure medicine and gone to bed, her thoughts flitting between the horrible encounter with Brett, the text from Win and her panicked guilt at not having said goodnight to Denny's ashes. It would be the first time since receiving the urn six months before that she'd not done so. At a certain point she got as far as sitting on the edge of the bed and feeling for her slippers on the carpet, but after a conflicted moment she fell back and lay across the bed sideways, unable to go downstairs and face her husband. He would never have spoken to Brett in the way she had, no matter how heartsick he felt at his son's sideways slide through life.

She slept very late and then could not get out of bed for an hour. At some point her cell phone buzzed: Win again. *Hey. You OK?* She thought for twenty minutes before clumsily tapping out her reply—*OK*—and shutting the phone off. The rest of the day went by in a blur; she forgot to eat until nearly three. But that evening she spent many quiet hours with Denny's ashes, finally curling up on the couch and falling asleep a few yards away from him, hoping against hope that he had forgiven her for Brett, for Win, for all she might have done wrong since his passing.

It did not embarrass her to admit that her late husband had been a better person than she. In fact, it gave her a feeling of pride at having chosen so well. Denny was an inspired architect whose work could be found all over San Francisco and far beyond; in a long career every single one of his designs had actually been built, a record that left his peers in awe. His clients included the Hollywood illuminati, a Google vice president, a trio of Singapore Airlines executives, an ex-President and, much to his gratification, a housing cooperative through which he had designed first homes for a hundred families. Denny worked relentlessly, but never let work intrude on his family time; in the final push of a project he would rise at three-thirty to squeeze more hours from the day, nodding off after dinner but doing so in the company of his wife and children.

She'd met him through her sister June, an accountant with his firm, and was dazzled by his clear green eyes, his reputation, and his bohemian aura. He wore peasant-style cardigan vests, jeans, and leather boots; he rolled his own cigarettes from a pouch of tobacco. She'd never dated anyone remotely like him. When he told her about the mentally retarded daughter who lived with him because his ex couldn't shake her drug habit—describing with genuine excitement how he'd taken Sonoma to the White House and Paris and Singapore in the course of his business travels, always accompanied by Mrs. Ramirez, the girl's tireless nanny— Helen was moved to tears. He asked her to marry him six months later. As they spoke their vows at the garden wedding Sonoma burst from her chair, chunky and awkward in her lilac dress, and rushed to give Helen a crushing hug, shouting *I do I do I do!* Helen was alarmed, but when she saw Mrs. Ramirez beaming at her she reminded herself that she'd known it wouldn't be easy, and thanked God there was a Mrs. Ramirez.

Nine years later, as she and Denny agonized over a counselor's recommendation that Sonoma be moved to a group home, Helen relived that first embrace and realized in the privacy of her heart that it no longer moved her as it once had. She saw now that Sonoma's affection was indiscriminate, a reaction to the moment, not focused on her at all. Only for Denny did Sonoma have an unwavering love. And now Brittany and Brett had begun to exact small cruelties against their demanding step-sister. All of them were exhausted. And so, at her urging, Denny finally abandoned his plan of keeping Sonoma with them for the rest of their lives. As the years went on Helen often wondered whether Denny was at peace with the decision—whether he missed the screaming embraces that had met him when he returned from work, the clumsy love—but he'd never revealed a trace of resentment to her, which was, after all, just like him.

The solution to the problem of Denny's ashes came to her unbidden on a Wednesday night. She was watching a PBS news show just to have some voices in the house; she found the stately diction of the moderator soothing in the manner of a spring thunderstorm too distant to be dangerous. A dull story about Wall Street gave way to a story about some activists who were ramming the boats of pirate whalers, and the screen filled with an ocean vista that seemed deeply familiar. She reached for the remote and turned up the volume. Just before the reporter said the words *Bodega Bay* she realized that the promontory was one Denny had taken her to see in the early years of their marriage and then at every opportunity thereafter. It was a short drive north of the forlorn little town on the California coast and a quick walk from the stone cottage Denny had shared with his first wife, Maya.

Though he was always careful in speaking of Maya, his passion for their battered pocket of coastline was unabashed. A radiant nostalgia came over him whenever they stood on the sturdy outcrop. He said without apology that it was the finest place he'd ever lived. It seemed not to occur to him that his second wife might wonder what portion of his happiness involved memories of her predecessor. Images of the young bohemians making love on the mossy turf, the rough sea cavorting far below, had been with her for so long that she took them for fact.

Now the reporter was interviewing a weathered salt who looked old enough to have served on the Pequod. Helen tuned him out. Not until the end of the story did the camera return to Denny's bluff, panning over a Pacific strewn with giant boulders gutted by the surf, the reporter's hair snapping in the wind. Helen knew exactly where the cameraman was standing, exactly how many steps it was to the precipice, exactly how the wind banked off the rocks and hammered up the cliff. This was Denny's place of pilgrimage. He had never been able to explain why it captivated him, but she sensed it had to do with youth and manhood and, probably, a companion who understood the power of the place better than she ever could have—a lover who still, somewhat unthinkably, lived in the stone house they'd shared.

Helen clicked the television off and sat very still.

She sat for a long while before having the courage to look across the room to Denny's urn. It sat ensconced in the warm light of a china lamp, radiating Denny's persistent silence, seeming to know what she was thinking. She went to it and cupped its rounded shoulder with her hand, at a loss for words, and went up to bed.

In the morning it occurred to her that she should not make the trip alone, and over the next hour, as she packed her things, she gradually realized who her traveling companion should be. She made a call and the arrangements were quickly made. By noon she was at the desk of the home's administrator, filling out paperwork, an old anxiety thumping in her chest. When the door opened and Sonoma came screaming toward her with her unruly joy Helen felt for an instant as if Denny were beside her, the true target, as always, of this strange woman's love. But it was she whom Sonoma embraced. *Mommy!* she cried, as if it were a challenge. *Mommy!*

Helen buckled Sonoma into the back seat of the Audi, struggling against her constant rocking. Denny's urn sat on the passenger-side floor, safely ensconced in a heavy flowerpot weighted with sand. As they merged onto 101 Helen took a deep breath, wishing for the first time in years that she had a cigarette, and Sonoma brayed out the question she knew was coming: *Are we going to see Daddy?*

She had not told her daughter of Denny's death because it seemed a cruelty to do so. Sonoma lived in the moment, everyone said; if so, could she really miss her father? Did she know whether she'd last seen him a day before or a year before?

Daddy's traveling, baby, she said, avoiding the hungry eyes in the rearview mirror.

As they crossed the bridge Sonoma's attention was drawn to the shimmering water below and the coppery towers above, and the car grew quiet. Here we are, Helen thought, the original three of us. As they crossed into Marin, Sonoma fell suddenly asleep, mouth open as if to drink in the sun. Helen felt an unexpected contentment slipping over her. She kept to the unpressured right lane until the turnoff toward the coast, then began the easy glide through the little hamlets with redwood needles washed like sea wrack along the shoulder of the narrow road.

As they neared the coast Sonoma started awake abruptly. Had she scented the ocean from the depths of her inscrutable sleep? Helen heard a snort from the back seat and saw her daughter struggle briefly against the shoulder strap, then sought out her brown eyes in the mirror, smiling. Helen surprised herself with that smile: something had shifted during the drive through the redwoods. Something had come free in her heart. Sonoma responded with a smile that engaged every muscle of her broad face. Helen nudged the buttons to roll both their windows down, flooding the car with the coastal perfume of verbena and redwood and the faintest tang of the sea.

Soon enough they came to the ragged outskirts of Bodega Bay, the crab shack and convenience store, the fishing squats and urgent care clinic, and Helen slowed down, picking her way along the narrowing curves. The place was not aging gracefully. Her daughter's large head lolled out the window now, luxuriating in the warm breeze.

Sonoma, honey, be careful. Come back inside the car.

In five minutes they'd broken through to the coast road. The vista of the level grey sea was unbroken now but for the wheeling gulls. There were sometimes whales spouting and breaching in the middle distance, but she couldn't recall the season. When did they migrate? She imagined showing them to Sonoma through binoculars, felt the simple joy it would bring, but the whales were gone. Then Helen recalled the seals tumbling in the filthy water below the pier. Sonoma would love to see them, would delight in their antics, but there was no time for diversions. Denny sat in his flowerpot beside her, his presence never stronger. While it sounded absurd to say that he might be somehow present in a heap of ashes, she couldn't deny that she felt him in the car, and had felt him in the living room every evening since his death. He was there in some way she didn't understand but couldn't doubt. Did he sense where they were now? That they were approaching the place he had most loved in his abbreviated life?

She wheeled around a last sloping curve and there it was: a gravel road splitting off and heading into the grassy dunes. A mass of blue lupine pointed the way. Helen turned into the side road too quickly and felt the car skid hard on the uncertain surface. For a moment she lost control completely. Sonoma screamed in the back seat as she pulled the car to an abrupt halt.

Are you okay, sweetie? Helen asked, leaning back to take her daughter's hand.

Fun! said Sonoma, her face aglow.

At this Helen laughed and eased back on the brake, letting the car amble into the dunes. A single gull swooped ahead like an unhurried pace car, starkly white against the pink thistle and yellow primrose that mingled with the sporadic grasses. The sea was behind them now, exerting a quiet pressure.

Helen negotiated a narrow bend in the road and came upon the house, just where she thought it would be: the humble stone cottage where Denny had lived so many years before. Whenever they would visit the promontory he'd point to the rutted access road and describe the way the house lay nestled in flower-filled dunes . . . the five-minute walk to the bluff . . . the old stone basin that still sat in the tidy yard. Though they'd never actually turned off and sought out the house, Helen recognized the place as if from memory.

She stopped the car in the road and sat for a long minute to take it in. The cottage was well-kept and sweet. She recognized a woman's touch: windowboxes overflowing with the same flowers that carpeted the dunes, prim white curtains in the kitchen windows. More than half the yard was given over to a large vegetable garden. Again Helen was aware of an unaccustomed peace opening beneath her, surely the last thing she'd expected to feel. Even Sonoma had grown placid. Perhaps it was the spirit of the place that stilled her, or Denny's deep love for it. Or perhaps again it was Denny's pleasure at being back. Helen looked over at the urn in its flowerpot and reached to lay her hand upon the smooth green lid. She had brought him home. She closed her eyes and slipped down in her seat, feeling time slow around her.

I thought you might show up one day, said a woman's voice at the open car window.

Helen opened her eyes with a start and there she was: Maya Weatherill, Denny's first wife.

She'd been gardening; a smudge of soil adorned her face like war paint gone dull. Her green eyes were perfectly clear, her skin weathered like a sailor's, her hips narrow as a teenager's in their banged-up overalls. A stretch of lean, tan flank showed where the denim parted. *But sixty*, Helen thought, *sixty if a day*.

Maya, she said.

Helen. Have you come to see me, or were you just passing by?

It seemed an absurd question to Helen, an aggressive one, but then she saw that Maya was smiling. Embarrassed, she smiled back.

Not exactly to see you, said Helen. More to invite you along.

Maya inclined her head and at the same moment a commotion broke out in the back seat. Sonoma was struggling with the shoulder belt, fidgeting like a child.

Mommy, she said sourly. I have to pee.

Helen watched Maya's gaze enter the car and find Sonoma. Maya took a step back from the door, a bright panic in her eyes.

My daughter, said Helen. Our daughter.

Oh, my god. Helen . . .

May we use your bathroom? It's best not to wait.

Of course, said Maya, stepping aside as Helen left the car and went back to release Sonoma, who was rocking hard now. Maya wrapped her thin arms around her fallen breasts and watched from a distance. When Sonoma stood before her at last she took a deep breath and held it for a long while.

Hello, Sonoma, she said with feigned cheer.

I have to pee, Sonoma repeated in her sing-song way. Have to pee, have to pee.

And so Maya led the way into the cottage, through the mud-room with its boot scraper and tall yellow Wellingtons, through the bright kitchen with its rough table and open fireplace, past the small peach-colored bedroom with a disorderly pile of books by the bed. In the space of twenty steps Helen knew that Maya was alone in life, a solitary woman growing old in the dunes. Sonoma marched straight into the bathroom—Helen wasn't aware that she'd learned to use the toilet by herself—and the two women heard the door lock. Maya sent Helen a questioning look; Helen shrugged.

Can I offer you some tea? Maya asked as they waited.

Thank you. I don't think so.

Maya pulled a rustic chair from the table and motioned for her guest to sit. From the bathroom came a series of groans and then the sound of a flushing toilet, in turn followed by a final and definitive grunt. The two women could not help but smile.

Does she still live with you? Maya asked.

No. It's a long story, but Denny and I decided that the right thing was to put her in a group home where she could have social contact with other women like her.

Was that a long time ago?

Some years.

Maya digested this information quietly, looking down at the table with a neutral gaze, but then met Helen's eyes. There were tears in her own.

Helen, I'm sorry I couldn't keep her. If you knew—

I think I understand. Denny shared enough with me that I get it. There's no ill feeling. It was so long ago.

But I was a terrible mother. A non-mother. It's unforgivable.

No one's blaming you but you.

At this moment the bathroom door burst open and Sonoma barreled triumphantly into the room. She walked straight to Maya and stood over her like a headmistress.

Who are you?

Well, she said uncertainly, seeking out Helen's eyes, I'm an old friend of your father's.

At this Sonoma instantly brightened. Oh! she cried, and gave Maya a powerful hug. Maya bore it for a wordless moment and then twined her arms around her daughter. But Sonoma broke free and stood bolt upright.

Where's Daddy? she demanded.

Maya threw Helen a pleading look. Honey, said Helen, I don't know if we'll get to see Daddy on this trip. Hey—would you two ladies like to go see the ocean?

Sonoma clapped her hands with glee. Maya was out of her chair and holding the door open for them before anyone could speak.

─────────

Wait, said Helen as they neared the Audi. I need to get something.

Reaching into the car, she lifted Denny's urn from its protective flowerpot and carefully closed the door with her hip. As always she was surprised at how light the urn was, but as she held it, it seemed to radiate a comforting warmth. She glanced up to see Maya's quizzical look, then a dawn of recognition. *Denny?* Maya mouthed silently. Helen smiled calmly.

C'mon, she said to Sonoma, lead the way. At this Sonoma strode out ahead, looked both ways down the gravel access road and turned left toward the sea, setting out with great aggressive steps.

Stop before the highway, honey, Helen called. Sonoma thrust a hand in the air to signal that she had heard.

Maya and Helen walked for a long moment in silence, Helen cradling the urn carefully, watching the road. Maya matched her stride, stealing a wary glance at the urn.

You know that Denny loved this place more than any other, don't you? asked Helen.

No, I didn't know that at all.

He did. He traveled all over the world but this is where his heart was happiest.

But . . . he had a whole happy life with you. You had children . . . he was so successful.

That's all true, but it doesn't change the fact that he never stopped dreaming of this place. Of what you two had here.

I don't know what to say, Helen.

You don't need to say anything. The most important thing is that we're here together. With Denny and our daughter.

The access road came to an end. Sonoma waited obediently at the edge of the coast road, rolling a yellow primrose in her big hands. Together the three of them crossed the road, Helen bringing up the rear with the urn folded safely in her embrace.

Keep clear of the edge, Sonoma! called Helen. Stay on the grassy part.

They stood on the promontory, gazing out at the sea. Down below, the Pacific threw itself against gnarled rocks scattered among the tidal pools, the blue water frothing and fizzing and bursting into the air as the combers barreled in. Gently Helen settled Denny's urn against a granite boulder overlooking the precipice, then returned to Maya's side.

Maya? she said uncertainly.

Yes?

How do you do it? I mean, it seems to me you've mastered this thing of living alone.

Maya considered this and smiled tiredly. Mastered it? I'm terrible at it. Despite decades of dedicated practice.

But you've made a real home.

A very lonely home. You can't imagine how still it is at night. How there are no voices. That's why I keep on living here. At least you hear the surf.

Helen nodded. For me it's public TV. I play the TV for the voices. Not as dignified as the ocean.

Let's walk. I'm worried about Sonoma over there. The path needs shoring up.

And so the two women walked along the bluff, the wind picking up. All at once Sonoma turned and ran toward them, full of joy, laughter pealing from her as she flew past.

She's so happy, said Maya, smiling. Her soul seems wide open.

And so does yours. Shall we sit?

They picked their way down to a patch of wiry grass nestled beneath an overhanging rock, a kind of sheltered retreat high above the water. Maya settled in and drew her long legs up to her chin. The flat horizon of the sea spread before them grandly. Below, the same sea harried away at the deadly rocks and the forlorn half-moon of sand. Helen stretched her legs out in the sun.

It took me forever to figure out what to do with his ashes, she said after a long while. I so much wanted to do what he would have wished . . . but I didn't know what that was. And then I thought of this place. And thought of you.

I can't believe your generosity. In including me, I mean.

He would have wanted it. I'm sure of it. Maybe he wants it now. I have this feeling that he's here, aware, with us. But I know what that sounds like.

We don't know anything. The older I get, the less I know.

At this the two women shared a quiet laugh and fell silent for a long while, until Maya suddenly got to her feet.

It's too quiet. Where's Sonoma?

On instinct Helen scanned the rocks below, the breakers, the beach, but there was no sign of trouble. Maya was already climbing back up onto the narrow path, taking the jagged rocks with a sure stride. It was as Helen reached the foot of the path that she saw Maya scramble deftly onto a granite ledge and look away from the sea in the direction Sonoma had run. In the face of her daughter's joy Helen had not realized that she was running past them toward the coast road. In ten bounding strides she caught up with Maya, who stood on the granite overhang five feet above the path.

Maya! Helen shouted up.

Come, said Maya, crouching to reach a hand down. There was an odd calm about her, a certain distance. Helen scrambled up the incline, Maya's hand gripping her forearm, and when she reached the ledge she saw tears in the clear green eyes. Together the two women stood and Maya pointed not at the road but farther out along the promontory, past the turnout where Helen and Denny would park to watch the sea.

At the very cusp of the precipice, at the very edge of the continent, stood their daughter Sonoma, her face upturned toward a solitary daytime moon they had not noticed until that moment. Helen felt her legs starting to give way and clutched Maya's hand to steady herself. As they watched, Sonoma closed her eyes and seemed to scent the air, slowing time to a crawl. Her two mothers stopped breathing as one, unable to move or speak. A gull cawed high above, the sound reverberating briefly until the surf rolled in to smother it. It was then that the two women saw their wayward daughter pirouette clumsily on her small rocky stage and, with a great curving swing, sow her father's ashes out over the Pacific. At first the ashes described a lovely arc, angling gracefully down toward the water. But then an updraft caught the fine powder and lofted it back toward Sonoma, the soft caress of it on her face making her squeal with joy, and reaching down hungrily she scooped another handful from the urn and released it into the wind, inventing a new and thrilling game with the man who had never been too tired to care for her happiness.

Not Yet

The summer of Walker's folly was one of the driest on record, a brutal season that had already felled hundreds of cattle by the time June was out. At night the skies were skeined with useless heat lightning; by day they transmitted a heat so intense it melted candles on dining room tables, even up in the mountain homes. The truck farms out on the plains were in deep trouble, acre after acre of sweet corn and sugar beets laid low, the aquifers beneath the land all but played out. It could only seem cruel that when the rains finally came they should take the form of a brief, freakish hailstorm, a cataclysm so violent it jerked potatoes out of the dirt and flung them aside like pulled teeth.

Yet in this parched summer, so desolate of relief, Charles

Walker was more and more convinced that he was in love. It was his third summer alone, and the first since Maggie's passing that had felt like a summer as he understood summer to be: a time of slowed obligation, a time to forget one world and recall, gradually, another. The students were gone—the early morning lectures and the afternoon office hours during which he found himself cloistered, more and more often it seemed to him, with dreary kids who needed psychotherapy more than a chat with their English professor. They would come in to talk about Hawthorne or Poe or Melville and within minutes would be in tears, the weight of their tenuous worlds pouring out in confessions he felt ill-equipped to receive. Embarrassed, Walker would simply listen, restless and conscious of the clock, wanting to get past the awkward interviews and back out into the welcoming spring air.

It was around the time of Maggie's diagnosis that he began to notice a change in his body, something he worried might mean medical trouble but that turned out to be only one of the indignities of late middle age. As some well-scrubbed Elizabeth or Rebecca would sit in the hard chair recounting her latest breakup or describing her awakening as a lesbian, Walker would realize that his bladder was suddenly and quite urgently full. There seemed no decent way to interrupt the heartfelt monologue so that he might attend to matters. And so he would sit like a scolded boy forced to hold it, the office too warm, water whooshing through the pipes intolerably. When he was finally released to hurry to the washroom the torrent would threaten to begin before he reached the urinal. Washing his hands at the sink afterward, he would look candidly at his heavy eyelids and spotted skin and fail yet again to find any dignity whatsoever in aging: it was simple loss, a sort of evisceration that made him angry.

Wasn't it only a year or two since he'd taken private pleasure in the way some of his female students—always the bookish, unlovely girls with whom he felt a secret kinship—flirted with him? Yet this had stopped now as if by unspoken decree. And no wonder: when he saw his photo in the new faculty directory he saw a grandfatherly man, approachable because sexless—a man who struggled to contain his urge to urinate, whose legs balked at the trudge up University Hill; in short, a man on the cusp of old age. What he had always assumed would be a gradual diminution had turned out to be a sudden step down, a stumble, and this alarmed him deeply.

It seemed to be happening to Maggie too. An avid tennis player, she reported one evening that she was finding it hard to reach the net when Louise, a friend of twenty years, lobbed a drop shot her way. Seeing this opening, Louise exploited it, and Maggie felt betrayed to the point of tears. There was a strange weakness in her legs, she confessed to Walker over dinner, a sluggish feeling that did not sort with the fact that she was walking three miles a day and making the circuit of the machines at the YMCA several times a week. She should have been stronger on the court than ever, but she could not keep up, and it was all slipping away very fast.

The weakness was sometimes interrupted by spasms that overtook her arms and legs at unpredictable times. The first had occurred one night after they made quick work of a lobster, coming on so fast that she screamed in panic. Her forearms would lock rigidly as if bound to her upper arms with steel cable; her fists would clench and roll forward like primitive, club-like hooves, useless to her for long despairing minutes. She thought of the posters of kids with cerebral palsy that seemed to have been everywhere in her childhood years—always doe-eyed kids in wheelchairs, gesturing weirdly with their spastic arms. Was this to be her fate too?

Soon there was even worse news. Maggie realized that she was losing her eyesight at an alarming rate. Quite suddenly—in a matter of weeks, it seemed—she found herself unable to make out signs or judge the distance of oncoming cars. She had never needed glasses, but now the morning newspaper was an unintelligible blur. Tennis became even more difficult and then unthinkable. One afternoon, disgusted at her inability to read the label on a cereal box in the grocery store, she stopped at the optometry booth and was told that her vision had declined to 20/50; between January and May her right eye had plummeted to 20/200 and the optometrist sternly ordered her to consult an ophthalmologist, who informed her that if her left eye were to follow suit she would be legally blind.

Blind!

How could it be? Less than a year ago it had been she who read the fine print for her astigmatic husband. The doctor told her that there was a laser surgery option that might help, but in the next breath advised her to see a neurologist. Feeling contrarian, she bought three pairs of the strongest readers she could find and instead made an appointment with her primary care physician, who told her the same thing: see a neurologist, and quickly.

Apparently the rate of her decline was suspiciously steep. The young neurologist, prematurely balding and dressed casually in a golf shirt and khakis, took down her story carefully and then examined her as Walker sat with fingers interlaced in his lap. She was worried for her husband: whatever the news turned out to be, they both knew that she would be better able to cope with it than he would. The exam moved through its paces. When the doctor grasped Maggie's fingers and pushed them backward, asking her to resist the pressure, she was helpless to comply. This led to other tests which proved that her weakness was real and considerable. As they composed themselves to hear his verdict, the doctor glanced toward a box of tissues, a gesture that impressed her—what tact—but also terrified her. She took a tissue and used it to polish her drugstore glasses as he told them that the results of her exam were inconclusive and then briefed them on the next steps—an MRI, a spinal tap and some other, less familiar tests. As he talked on, it occurred to her, with perverse irrelevance, that the blurriness of his face made his voice more distinct, like a voice from a radio.

She asked what might be causing her symptoms and the diseases he mentioned were without exception frightening. At the words *multiple sclerosis* she felt Walker recoil in his chair as if dodging a blow; at the words *a mass, what we would commonly call a tumor* he swallowed so loudly that the doctor stopped speaking for a moment. There were also some "real outliers" that needed to be ruled out, he added, but the odds were so low that it wasn't worth discussing them at this early stage in their studies. He paused and asked if they had any questions for him. She looked over at Walker but couldn't read his expression. Honey? she asked, unable to get a word out of him. She was sure they would think of a hundred questions the minute they left the clinic. As she lowered herself from the exam table she lost her balance and would have fallen had the doctor not deftly intercepted her.

Maggie trundled dutifully through the round of tests, the dread spinal tap turning out to be a nothing, painless save for the headache that came afterward. When the results came in they were a surprise even to the doctor. As they sat in the same brightly lit exam room he reviewed the various lab reports and concluded that all the more common diseases would have to be ruled out in favor of one of the "outliers" he had alluded to. It was her bad fortune, apparently, to be suffering from neuromyelitis optica, a fairly rare disease in which the body attacks its own optic nerves and spinal cord. The blindness, the spasms, the weakness all made sense; what Charles and Maggie could not make sense of was the prognosis. The course of the disease was wildly variable, with outcomes ranging from mild impairment to death by asphyxiation due to destruction of the spinal nerves that fed the diaphragm. How could such opposite extremes be made to coincide?

That night they cried together for the first time since the stillbirth of their one child thirty years before—she almost silently and Walker, to the surprise of them both, in great bawling sobs. When the grief subsided she went to the basement pantry and resurfaced with the best bottle of wine in the house, their special occasion bottle, and with some difficulty cranked it open. Walker watched her from the depths of his armchair, too confused to speak, until she put the glass in his hand and leaned over to kiss him, steadying herself against his shoulder.

Carpe diem, Charles, she said. Life is shorter than we ever think it's going to be.

She would be dead before summer came. Determined to master her body's frailty, she had started hiking nearly every day in the foothills, setting out in the early morning so that the sun's slant would throw her shadow ahead of her. Her shadow was her silent guide and protector, a hiking companion who helped orient her to the murky trail and would rise up before her if an obstruction loomed ahead. The mild slope was brutal for her now, and as the heat of the day began to drill down her legs grew even weaker. Yet she kept at it with defiance.

There was a clearing midway up the path with a flat rock that cantilevered out over the town, and here she would take a short rest, stretching her weary legs and gulping water noisily, her swallowing thick and labored of late. She could make out nothing of the town below but shapeless pools of color; the panorama of downtown shops and the faux-Tuscan roofs of the university might as well have been the dappled hide of an animal. But she enjoyed the faint breeze, the lucid mountain air, the solitude, and felt a small sense of accomplishment as she sat on her old rock day after difficult day.

It was on a Thursday morning in late May, while her husband was conducting a lethargic seminar on the Transcendentalists, that Maggie settled herself in her aerie and reached for her water bottle only to find that she had forgotten it. (So much Charles would surmise later, when he discovered the bottle standing by the door.) The sun was already blazing and she must have been unbearably thirsty, her body aching for water. As she sat bathed in sweat under the unforgiving sun she may have felt a strange distraction, as if she were watching herself from a few steps away— and this would have been her last sensation before an epileptic seizure took her in its grip. They found her crumpled on the patio of a house three hundred feet below, mutilated by a merciless fall down the rocky hillside, her lovely face stained with blood gone ochre in the hot sun. The first-grader who discovered her fell mute for two weeks from the shock of it.

At first there was some question of suicide, but the autopsy was conclusive. She had been severely dehydrated, an affront that her compromised nervous system could not withstand. The seizure had come quickly and the force of it had caused her to roll or hurtle off the rock to her death—a death whose sudden drama could not have been further from the proudly undramatic way in which she'd lived her life.

Maggie would not have known what was happening, her doctor said, but this did not spare Walker his crippling grief—itself a disease that metastasized, within days, into an engulfing self-hatred. When the memorial was done and the lawyers and bureaucrats were finished with their paperwork he took leave from the university and retreated to the little cabin they'd kept up in the high country, resisting friends' admonitions that he should not be alone. Perhaps they were right, but he and Maggie had spent fifteen summers there; it might ground him to be there. If his new lot was to be alone, it might as well be in a place whose views of the valley and austere Half-Jack Mountain never failed to give solace.

As he walked the campus despondently during finals week it seemed that every third person he passed felt the need to stop and offer condolences, and this too made him want to get away. The good wishes of others only proved his new condition of otherness, his separation from the herd like the wounded and dangerous animal that he was. So on the Saturday after finals week he packed his things and headed up the canyon, turning into the rutted drive and dreading the sight of the bank of narcissus Maggie had developed, over a period of years, along the flagstone path leading to the front door. This too, this panged agony, was part of his new condition, like a dogged reminder of a disease that might one day kill him.

As the days lagged on he went about the old routines of summer—the morning coffee on the patio that overlooked the rocky maw of the canyon, the trudge down to the cold stream in search of trout, the afternoons spent rereading *Moby-Dick* in his annual tradition. One of his graduate students, a Colombian woman whose intuition was pitch-perfect, had given him a slim volume of poetry by the eighth-century Chinese hermit Han-shan; this he would sit and read on the porch in the endless evenings, a cup of strong coffee at his side and the deeply lowing canyon before him, trying to find comfort in the unruffled words of a man who, like him, had no one to talk to as evening wore into night. *My heart is like the autumn moon,* said Han-shan with his unaccountable joy—but the old hermit, Walker knew, had not lost Maggie. His own case was entirely different.

In the morning he would awake irritated rather than charmed by the thousand birds in the pines, wishing to be left to sleep forever. There were many days when he found that reading was simply impossible, and instead sought solace by dragging his weathered Adirondack chair into the back yard and tying flies in the sun, a lost fisherman marooned in a sea of weeds.

It was not until the third summer, the summer of the crippling drought, that things began to improve. Under the steady influence of Myra Hartung, the athletic, upbeat therapist he'd consulted off and on through the school year, he had begun to take what she called reintegrative steps. He invited friends for dinner, catering the evenings from the local gourmet shop; over Christmas break he tagged along on a study vacation to Stratford, gorging himself on Shakespeare and allowing himself to fantasize, in his hard B&B bed, about the young women who were sharing a bed next door. But most surprising of all was the change he wrought on his body. He began to take long walks that on the weekends gave way to long hikes, pushing himself to strengthen his legs and keep going whatever the weather, rewarding himself at the end not with his customary glass of wine and bachelor pasta but with a tall ice water and a plate of the quinoa salad and tarragon chicken he had discovered at the organic deli. He slept well and awoke with more energy than he'd felt in years. By spring Walker was reading nutrition books and taking a yoga class. He still missed Maggie terribly—the way she would tuck her chin between his head and shoulder in bed, the faintly floral scent of her, the bottomless well of stories they had shared after thirty years of marriage—but he knew he had turned a corner, and when he drove up to the cabin that June the fat paperback he threw onto the dashboard was not *Moby-Dick* but a guide to fifty high-country hiking trails.

Summer roared in with a dangerous heat, scalding the high pastures and bringing severe water troubles to the town below. It had been a strangely dry winter; with the spring thaw the shallow snowpack below the Isabelle Glacier yielded only a fifth of its normal meltwater, starving reservoirs that in a normal year would rise by the height of a man. Walker roamed his mountain roost shirtless, staying out of the stunning glare, annoyed that he could not keep up his exercise routine. The sun was so hot that the very act of breathing pained the lungs. Even the geckos on the garden's retaining wall were immobilized as if glued in place, panic obvious in their darting eyes.

June was a loss; but in early July the relentless assault abruptly ended, chased off by a temperate breeze that sluiced down through the foothills from somewhere up in Canada. One morning Walker awoke to springlike weather, as if the seasons were running in reverse, and spent the day puttering around the property in a state of quiet relief, weeding Maggie's beds, repairing a leaky hose, mucking out the fire pit. At six he settled himself on the porch with a plate of steamed vegetables and chicken, content to enjoy the gradual close of the day.

It was as he was finishing his supper that he heard the snort of a horse. The animal was close by; soon its long elegant face came around the side of the shed where a trail led into a stand of lodgepole pine. The horse shook its head to rid itself of a blackfly and the reins slapped gently against the muscular neck. In the next instant Walker saw the reins being laid to the horse's left, and the big animal obediently veered away from the cabin and back toward the woods.

The rider was a woman of perhaps thirty-two who smiled apologetically at Walker as she steered the horse away. Sorry for the intrusion! she called, but before he could reply she was gone, loping back into the pines with her cropped copper hair and leather chaps and perfect posture. She might have been an apparition, so fleeting was her irruption into his world. But he thought of her for hours and dreamed of her that night. He had seen her face for only an instant but there was a graceful firmness in it that stayed with him.

Slowly it occurred to Walker that the rider's quick retreat might have been less from a fear of disturbing his privacy than an unwillingness to disturb her own. He thought he sensed a solitariness in her, and this intrigued him as much as the sheaf of red hair, the firm hips and wide-splayed legs, the long and graceful back. For the first time since Maggie's death he pondered another woman without a voice inside him commenting on his foolishness.

It was three days before he saw her again. He was hiking down to the creek with his fishing tackle and a few pieces of fruit, not intending to stay long. Walker fished less now because he preferred to be in motion, but he still enjoyed the solitude, the play of current against his waders, the coolness of the stream under the day's heat. The trail led down through a fragrant pine forest, starting wide and then narrowing as it wove down toward the bank; he knew there was poison ivy at a particular spot and expertly sidestepped it, detouring along a rock outcrop, pleased by his new sense of balance. He was light on his feet, a more confident hiker than he'd been in years. The new strength in his legs still delighted him at times.

Walker had noticed how the drought expressed itself through a change in the voice of the creek. It was quieter now, thrushier, lacking the special crackle of cold water shattering itself against submerged stones. There were other signs of trouble too. About a hundred feet before the water's edge, for example, lay a swale that in an ordinary year would be marshy, impossible to cross without getting mired; now it was just a desiccated pitch of dirt that gave off a fetid odor. A quarter mile downslope there was a watershed where the mountain flow split into two strands, one weaving down through the canyon to feed the town's reservoirs, the other slipping into an alpine lake of great stillness and beauty. He had hiked around the lake several times and knew from its depressed level that there would be water trouble down in town, but this fact did not especially move him. Nor did the depredations of the pine beetles, relentless deep-borers that had turned a third of the forest into rust-brown tinder. He was content to let nature take its course.

What mattered lately was to observe with precision rather than to judge for good or ill. Perhaps it was Han-shan who had taught him this, perched on his own mountain watching the light change and the seasons come and go. Walker picked his way down to the creek in a state of high awareness and a certain peace, aware of magpies and busy scurryings in the brush and the loose progress of the water below.

At the bottom of the path the terrain eased into level ground that formed a margin along the creek, running downstream for a mile or so before disappearing into a stand of aspen. It was a good place for kayakers to put in and a good place for a fisherman to wade out. Walker's habit was to don his waders, work his way out into the current and then head upstream, well above the clearing, to avoid human traffic that might disrupt the concentration of the trout or tamper with his solitude. This he now did. With the reduced current the submerged rocks were more slippery than usual, less well scrubbed. Walker proceeded carefully, taking his time, until he reached a conjunction of tumbled boulders that he knew to be an ideal casting point.

It was as he made his first cast that he saw her. Amid the brush there was a small clearing marked by a flat rock overlooking the creek, and here she sat, her horse standing patiently in the woods behind her. When Walker spotted her she was assuming a difficult yoga pose, legs split in a hurdler's stance, torso a backward curve that threw her reaching arms behind her so that they were almost parallel to the ground. Walker had done just enough yoga to be impressed. But what took his breath away was the fact that she wore no clothes. In an instant he took in the taut line of muscle running along the tanned belly, the powerful shoulders, the breasts eased back by gravity along the plane of her reaching arms. He saw that she was breathing with her whole body, while he himself was not breathing at all. He stood watching her openly, immodestly, as the current brushed over his legs and his line was carried downstream toward a destination that no longer mattered.

She held her pose for several long minutes, then unwound it gradually into another. The new pose revealed more of her—the rest of her—and had he not been standing amid moving waters Walker might have sat down just to steady himself. Again she held her pose for a long while, then stood and turned toward the creek with hands folded and eyes closed, directly facing him. He looked away, sensing that at any moment she would discover the old voyeur before her and panic, but he could not resist turning back to look at her. Only twenty feet separated him from the loveliest thing he had seen in a very long time.

She made a half-bow and opened her eyes. It took a moment for her to notice him out in the creek, but when she did so she seemed almost unsurprised. Instinct made her turn away for a heartbeat, but then she turned back toward him, facing him unabashed, and gave him a wave and a smile.

Catching anything? she called.

He couldn't find his voice. By way of answer he sent her an ineffectual wave that made her laugh. Reaching into the bushes, she retrieved a flowered sarong and wrapped it around her waist.

Better?

Still he could not speak. Laughing again, she unknotted the sarong and rearranged it so that it covered her breasts as well. What about now?

I'm sorry, he said quietly.

I can't hear you!

Sorry, he called out, deeply embarrassed.

Don't be. I'm not.

Walker nodded, busying himself with his fly rod.

So—catching anything?

Not yet, he whispered.

Come closer. I can't hear you, said the woman, cupping her hand to her ear.

And without knowing what was happening to him—his legs somehow finding their way across the precarious spill of submerged rocks and algae—Walker made his way into her world.

———

She said her name was Linda, but something in her tone made him doubt it. He could hardly blame her if she chose to conceal her identity from this man who had trespassed onto her privacy.

Isn't this a perfect spot? she asked as they sat on her flat rock, taking the sun. I adore the solitude.

Until some old fisherman shows up.

Not every intrusion is an unwelcome one, she replied coolly. He let the comment float in the air and slowly settle onto the warm rock. The horse shook its withers softly behind them, near the little red dome of her tent—for she was camping here, another solitary in retreat, the sound of the water and the blaze of the stars lulling her to sleep every night.

How long have you been coming up here? she asked after a leisurely pause. How long have you had your place?

Some years now. Fifteen or so.

Oh, wow. That's such a nice spot. You've got the woods and you're so close to the national forest.

Yes, we're lucky.

At this Linda inclined her head in an unspoken query.

I bought the place with my late wife.

I am so sorry.

No worries, he said, instantly annoyed with himself for waving off three decades with Maggie—and for having done so with that stupid phrase all the kids now used.

Perhaps it was this slip, but suddenly the whole situation unnerved him. Look, he said, don't you think it's strange that you see this guy in the creek and just invite him over? With you naked? How do you know I can be trusted? I mean, I can be, but how would you know?

She smiled coyly. I don't know, entirely, but I know enough about you to have a pretty good idea you're not a monster.

What? What do you know about me?

I know that you have a passion for Melville, for example.

A distant alarm went off in the back of Walker's mind. Had she entered the cabin while he was gone? But no: this summer, for the first time in years, he had made the conscious decision not to bring his dog-eared *Moby-Dick*. There was no Melville to be found.

How in the world do you know that?

You were a very passionate teacher, Professor Walker. You talked about Melville like he was a god.

Walker stopped breathing. He realized that he was gaping at her and quickly closed his mouth.

Again the laugh came, but this time it was accompanied by a hand on his knee.

Got you, said Linda.

It seemed she had been his student more than a decade before, in her senior year at the university; one autumn she'd read Melville and then Henry James under him, struggling to keep up because she was such a slow reader. That was mostly what she remembered of the course—the hours and hours spent ploughing through Melville's supercharged prose and the tedious sentences of *The Ambassadors*, always running behind. But she also remembered, fondly, how Professor Walker would arrive for the one o'clock class carrying a grease-stained bag with a Polish sausage and proceed to devour it as he listened to one of the students read aloud from the day's novel, for this was how he felt any discussion of a serious writer should begin. This homely detail Linda had carried with her for years now.

Thanks a lot, he told her. Now you've given me a craving for a Polish and I can't fulfill it.

It looks to me like you don't allow yourself that kind of eating anymore.

Walker clasped his knees in his hands, looking away. It's true, he said, I try to eat better than that.

You look very well for a man your age.

Walker felt a lightness in his chest even as he waved off the compliment. Not bad for a grandpa, he continued silently, on Linda's behalf.

Not bad at all, she said, as if having read his thoughts.

If there was a beginning to his folly, this was the moment. All that evening he would go over her words in his mind, probing for nuance and concluding, despite himself, that she had been flirting with him. The memory of her tawny body on its solitary rock would not let go of him. Nor would the memory of her ease when she discovered that he was admiring her from his vantage point out in the creek. He didn't remember her from her student days—an awkward but unsurprising fact—but it didn't matter: her fond memory of him had been connection enough for her to invite him over to her rock. Walker fell asleep that night imagining how it might feel to bury his face in the sheaf of her coppery hair, and in the morning he decided to invite her to share the beautiful peaches he had bought in town the Saturday before. Sitting before him in the morning sun, they were as charged with symbolism as any peaches gathered by Madame Cézanne, and after breakfast he set out for her camp.

She was tidying her tent when he arrived. Good morning, he called. Did you sleep well?

She turned with delight in her green eyes, or so it seemed to him.

Marvelously! It's impossible not to sleep well here. You should come down off your hill and try it some time.

I may do just that. Listen, I don't want to disturb you but I nabbed some gorgeous peaches at the market and I can't possibly eat all of them. Would you like to come by later and enjoy them with your old professor?

Linda regarded him silently for a long while, her intelligent eyes making a careful study of the hopeful face before her, the boyish shock of hair gone white now but for a lone streak of gold.

Do you have any ice cream? she asked finally.

Vanilla, he lied. The perfect thing.

Well, then, that's an offer a girl can hardly refuse.

Come by after dinner, but before it gets dark.

Walker headed back up the hill toward the cabin, then drove down into town so that he could buy a gallon of vanilla ice cream and a pair of port glasses. He had decided during the uphill trudge that this would be the night, at last, to break into the prized 1977 Warre's he and Maggie had lugged to the cabin summer after summer but had never had the nerve to open. They'd bought the bottle years ago in a moment of recklessness—the hundred dollars a king's ransom then—and had lived in fear of it ever since. But Walker realized that its time had come at last, and as he eased through the switchbacks down the mountain he turned the radio off the better to construct an image of the evening, and the night to follow, in his mind.

——— ———

She arrived in fine form, making an entrance worthy of Guinevere. As he was puttering around the side yard in the early dusk, building a small teepee of kindling and pine logs in the fire pit, he heard two thumps and saw her horse standing at the edge of the woods, stamping its hoof as if to announce her entrance. She sat atop the tall animal with great dignity, watching Walker with a smile. He wondered how long she had been there, quickly replaying his own actions in his mind to see if he might have done anything embarrassing.

Am I early? she called from her mount.

Right on time, he said, waving her in.

Linda cantered her horse to the lone aspen tree that stood west of the house and dismounted with grace. For evening attire she had chosen a pair of battered jeans and a loose white cotton shirt knotted at her narrow waist. As she walked toward him Walker was surprised to see that she was barefoot.

What about your boots? he asked.

I've got them if it gets cold, said Linda, nodding over her shoulder at the bulging saddlebag. She gave him a quick hug and kissed his neck as if having overshot his cheek. Walker felt a jolt of arousal at the unexpected roughness of her lips. She smelled faintly of pine sap, a deep and vernal scent.

He realized that he had reflexively laid a hand on her hip, his fingers coming to rest along the band of warm skin between jeans and shirt. Before he could withdraw it she turned slightly, drawing his index finger across her waist. It all happened in an instant, but to Walker the quick pas de deux seemed ripe with meaning.

Linda asked if he could scare up a bucket of water for Rona, who must, he guessed, be the horse—a mare, he now noticed. The English professor in him instantly made the connection: Rona was indeed a roan mare, her chestnut coat underlaid with white. The cleverness of the name spoke well of Linda.

Of course, he said, happy to have something to occupy his hands. Let's get Rona a drink and then let's get us one too.

On the porch's rugged table he had set out a blue platter piled high with the peaches, and here they settled with their drinks. The fruit truly was magnificent, trucked in from an orchard on the Utah border.

Those look every bit as delicious as you promised, she said, sipping her ice water, one denim knee tucked under the other on the beige Adirondack chair.

Want one now?

Let's watch the sunset first. Want to concentrate.

The canyon was filling with shadows like a quarry filling with rain. To the west the sun teetered on a crag, the naked granite splaying its light in all directions. It was a moment he knew well, having shared it with Maggie year after year; this summer he had made it a nightly rendezvous, one of the few anchor points of his solitary life. And now a new woman was here to share it with him. They fell silent, hands curled around their respective drinks, and watched the evolving dusk, a trio of red-tailed hawks wheeling above and Rona snorting diffidently in the yard.

When the darkness came, it came suddenly. One moment she was sitting beside him in vivid profile; in the next she vanished into the utter blackness of the moonless mountain night. He fought the urge to take her hand.

Well, she said after a while, I guess night has fallen. Decisively. It happens so fast up here.

I'm a little chilled, Charles. Not sure about the ice cream idea. I think I'll get my boots.

And I thought I might light a fire in the pit.

Splendid, she said with mock formality, brushing past him in the darkness. He heard her step confidently down off the porch in the pitch-black night and then say something to the horse in a low voice. She and Rona had known each other a long while, she'd said: Rona had, in fact, been her college graduation gift. They seemed to share an intimate language.

Walker took a hurricane lamp and headed out to the side yard to light the fire. The tinder went up quickly—it had been so dry of late—and he extinguished the lamp, using a pine bough to brush old ashes off the stone rim of the pit.

Soon enough she came around the corner of the house, boots on her feet and her shirttails untied. She was hugging herself loosely. Charles, she said in a quiet voice, do you think I could borrow a sweater? I didn't dress very wisely for such an outdoorsy girl.

In short order he got her zipped into his bulky black fleece and sat her down next to him in front of the developing flames. Much better, Linda said contentedly, stretching her legs out and sinking into her chair. Again he could have reached over and taken her hand, but did not. The moment was sufficient unto itself: he had not felt so happy since long before Maggie's death, before her diagnosis and all that followed. One night early in the summer he had sat exactly here and tried to think back to the last moment of true happiness they had shared before her decline, but couldn't single one out; there was only the routine of life, the round of days, no clear threshold on whose far side lay a time of simple joy. It had troubled him that he could not remember such a time. Perhaps he and Maggie had been together too long for it, or perhaps not long enough; would he have felt the same happiness if it were her beside him rather than a young woman half his age? A cynical voice in him said no, but a kinder voice said perhaps so. Perhaps by now, had she survived, they would have entered a new phase of life in which such happiness again became possible. He would never know.

Sorry, said Linda after a time.

For what?

I think I'd like a peach, now that you're all comfortable.

There was enough firelight now to see her face, her lively green eyes. In the first frightening days of her illness Maggie had insisted that he find someone new when she died—she would not be talked out of the idea of her own impending death, though the prognosis was mixed—and he had always dismissed the idea, panic rearing in him. As he looked at Linda now he felt that Maggie was very near. She would not have blamed him for this happiness, he felt certain. The realization released a still greater joy and he smiled broadly at the young woman at his side.

Sit tight, he said, rising. A few minutes later he returned with a tray bearing the peaches and ice cream, bowls and spoons and a paring knife, the 1977 port, the two crystal glasses.

Peaches and port, he said, answering her coy smile.

Why, if that girl in your class ever imagined—

May I?

Walker peeled and pitted the best of the peaches for her as she watched, turning the slices out into the bowls and adding scoops of ice cream. As he worked he was conscious of his own calmness, the unhurried skill of his large hands, and knew that she noticed it too.

When she had finished savoring her dessert he took up the Warre's bottle. Port? he asked.

I don't really know much about port. Is this a good one?

No.

Linda frowned, thrown off balance for an instant.

This, said Walker, is not a good port; it is an excellent port. A 1977.

She paused pensively, then said: That's the year I was born, Charles. Did you know that?

Of course not. But that doesn't mean we have to assume it's just a happy accident, do we?

Walker confidently opened the bottle that had intimidated him for so many years. She watched him pour the first ruby-red drafts, fascinated. As he handed her a glass she took it and inclined her head toward him, a question preparing itself in her eyes.

Charles, she asked, how long have you had this bottle?

Why does it matter?

Because if you bought it this afternoon, that is lovely of you. But if you've had it for years, that is something else entirely.

In a good way?

I honestly don't know. I would have to question whether I'm quite worth it.

Walker regarded her with disbelief. Worth it? he said. This is the happiest I've been in years.

His words hung in the air, a naked declaration neither of them was prepared for. The fire popped, sending a curving hand of sparks into the night sky; Rona fussed beside her aspen tree. There was nothing more to be said, but Linda found the right words nonetheless:

Well, then I am happy for you.

With this she raised her glass and clinked it against his, the fire tumbling up into the night as they drank.

By the time Walker kissed her, half the bottle was gone and she was listing toward him in her chair, more than half asleep, the firelight burnishing her hair. As her head dropped toward him Walker noticed a tiny mole along her hairline, perhaps just a dark freckle, and it was this that snapped the last thread of his self-restraint. Taking her cheek in his palm, he raised her head gently and brought her rough lips to his.

At first she seemed not to notice, so close was she to sleep. If her lips responded faintly it was perhaps only from habit, not any special feeling for him. But at his second kiss she drew back and opened her eyes to find her old teacher very close indeed. Charles, she said, touching his cheek for a scant moment. Um—Charles. And with this she pulled away. She looked at him for a long while, her eyes unreadable. A wind had started to rise, lifting a strand of her hair and laying it gently across her face just as Walker might have done.

So, he said when he could wait no longer. What are you thinking?

She looked down into a glowing log, took three careful breaths and met his eyes calmly.

What am I thinking? I am thinking: Not yet.

Walker felt his heart sink and then rise again: Not yet, after all, was far from No. He could wait for her: he would wait for her, for as long as she needed him to.

Okay, he said, trying to smile. Not yet.

Before she said goodnight they shared another peach, dredging the slices in the melted ice cream and passing the bowl back and forth, not bothering with the second spoon. They sat for a while longer, watching the embers flare in the light wind, coyotes yipping in the woods: it was a perfect Western night, the sort they both loved deeply, and there was no need for words. Before mounting Rona for the ride back to her campsite Linda gave Walker an unfeigned hug and then kissed him on his mottled cheek, and it was this kiss that he spirited off to bed with him, this kiss that he dreamed of.

Deep in the night, Walker was awakened by the sound of an explosion. He stumbled through the dark to the bedroom window and was alarmed to see a tall pine at the edge of the yard engulfed in flames.

It was a tree he loved very much, for it was the tree under which Maggie had sat reading summer after summer, an iced tea on the flat armrest of the chair and a bowl of fruit balanced in the grass. She had read all of Proust there one year, serious-faced but occasionally laughing with delight; another summer she had marched through Churchill's history of the war, inevitably falling asleep in the late afternoon sun, the book spreadeagled below her breasts. But now Maggie's beloved tree was in flames. As Walker watched in confusion the tree next to it exploded with a smashing crack, flaring up like a struck match. He had no idea that a tree could explode. Suddenly the yard seemed a minefield.

Walker saw that a front of flame was quickly carving away

at the edge of the forest as if tracing Rona's hoofprints, making quick work of the dry pines. Already the path into the forest was a gauntlet of fire. In panic, Walker pulled on his pants and ran into the yard shirtless, his mind an organ of raw perception that took in the glaring blaze, the shocking heat, the roar of the forest being consumed. He could not think what to do. Pointlessly he began dragging the Adirondack chairs toward the house until he realized he was only racking more fuel against the wooden siding. He froze in mid-stride, frantic, unable to move.

The main front was moving away from him, carried on a wind that had risen considerably while he slept. But then the dry grass of the back yard began crackling, and in a matter of seconds a ground fire was grazing its way steadily toward the house. At the sight of it Walker's paralysis was broken. He flew to the garden hose and opened it full bore onto the yard, curtains of steam rising where the water hit the low flames. But the wind was sweeping the grassfire toward him too rapidly. In the course of one or two minutes it became obvious that anything he could do would be futile.

And so Walker ran back into the house, threw a shirt on and took up his car keys. He wondered with a sudden pang if Linda was all right. The blaze was striking into the woods in the direction of the creek; if he could get down the main road there was a turnout from which it was only a short walk to the water's edge. Walker threw the Volvo in gear and swept onto the pitted road, the conflagration at his back and the air thick with smoke. The thought of losing the cabin made him sick to his stomach but he tried to put it out of his mind: he knew now that he must get Linda out of harm's way.

There was a bend in the road that looked back at the mountain, and when Walker reached it the full extent of the inferno was revealed. A jagged front of orange flame and white smoke was boiling over the edge of the national forest, the tall lodgepole pines shooting up plumes of fire twice their height and the neighboring trees throwing back an intense glow. To the east, the flames were marching straight for a pocket of expensive homes tucked down in the next canyon. Walker could hear the sound of the stalking creature through his open car window, an animal roar that seemed to come from the ground itself. Startled by the sheer volume of it, he gunned the engine and kept driving. There was not another soul on the road.

When Walker reached the turnout he threw the car into park. The fire was on the near horizon, clearly visible through a break in the trees, the wind pushing the tips of the flames in his direction. He could not tell how fast it was moving. Walker hesitated for a moment, weighing the risk of being trapped on the mountain, but the thought of Linda pinned down by the river sent him into furious action. He made for the trailhead and plunged into the darkness of the forest, the brush thick enough to cut off the livid glow.

Why had he not thought to bring a flashlight? He stumbled down the steep trail like a drunken man, mostly guessing at the terrain underfoot and certain he was about to twist an ankle. But after some minutes the path leveled out and he knew he was coming to the creek. He began to call her name, trudging upriver toward the clearing where she had pitched her tent. Every few steps he would stop and listen, but what he heard was the rumble of the inferno and now, at last, the sound of sirens—never her voice. It seemed to him that the flames could not be far off but there was no way to know for certain. They might reach him in an hour, or in ten minutes. He went on calling her name, wondering in the back of his mind what had become of the cabin with its wall of books, its carved bedstead, its collection of Navajo blankets. By now it must be engulfed, perhaps already rendered down to ash.

Maggie! Walker cried out, startling himself. At the sound of her name he felt Maggie to be very near, hovering at his side in a way he could not grasp, neither spirit nor flesh. In the distance a muffled explosion sounded and he spotted Linda's flat rock a dozen yards in front of him.

When he reached the clearing he found her tent intact, but no sign of Rona or Linda. Walker knelt and opened the tent flap. Inside lay a sleeping bag, a flashlight and a copy of *Desert Solitaire*, but no Linda. Walker stood up and called her name in all directions, but the mounting sound of sirens made it hard to hear anything else. It occurred to him that she might be out looking for him just as he was looking for her. And so he crashed through the brush and scrambled back up the hill to his car, wheeling it about and heading up the flank of the burning mountain.

Smoke barreled into his headlights now, pouring down from the blaze. Blinded, he switched to his low beams as the reek of it began to invade the Volvo. His eyes began to sting and then to water profusely. Walker switched on the air conditioner and punched the recirculation button, pushing up the mountain into the thickening smoke. He could no longer see the edge of the road. Counting on his memory to keep the wheels on the gravel, Walker downshifted into second and urged the car up the steepening grade. *Not yet*, he heard Linda say again. He had kissed her and she had said *Not yet*, which did not mean *Never*.

There were sirens everywhere now, a commotion of emergency response. As he rounded a switchback he met a chaos of gunning engines and flashing blue lights. Less than an hour had passed since he'd been awakened by the exploding tree in his back yard, but now it seemed the whole canyon was on the move. Walker's headlights punched through the smoke to reveal a compact yellow fire engine blocking the road ahead. As he stopped the Volvo a sharp siren squawk and a sputter of red lights overtook him from behind. He heard a door slam and then a sheriff's man was rapping on his window, his big hand holding a surgical mask over his face. Walker rolled the window down and smoke poured into the car. Ahead, the fire engine gunned its motor and vanished into the murk.

You got to get off the mountain! shouted the deputy through his mask. You're blocking this road.

I have a house up there.

Anyone home?

No, said Walker. Then: Maybe. There may be.

The deputy regarded him skeptically. So, he said, is there someone home or do you just want to get back up there to save your stuff?

Linda may be there. I've got to get through, Officer.

Linda's your wife?

Girlfriend.

At this the deputy produced a walkie talkie and asked for Walker's address, relaying it to the dispatcher. Ten-four, said a voice through the static. Well-being check at 122 Bentwood.

They'll make sure she's all right, if she's there, said the deputy. Now turn around and get down off this mountain before things get any worse.

Walker nodded and rolled up his window, intending to comply, but when he put the Volvo into gear something made him pull past the officer and head up the mountain. *Not yet*, she'd told him. *Not yet*, he said aloud in the car. *Not yet!*

Walker was distantly aware of red lights flashing behind him but thought of them as a kind of receding fare-thee-well, a festive display. The smoke was thickening dramatically and he began to cough. An amber glow blanketed the canyon to his left, but as the car rounded a steep curve the glow reared up before him in a virulent orange curtain. The whole mountain was on fire, flames charging up the steep slope in swaths hundreds of yards wide and then converging near the crest like victorious battalions. The terrible immensity of it took Walker's breath away. He lifted his foot from the gas, gawking at the destruction before him, and in this moment the police car spun past to block his path. The deputy was out of the car and flinging the Volvo's door open in a heartbeat. A solid fist of heat struck Walker squarely in the face as the outside air rolled in.

I told you to get off the mountain, sir, shouted the deputy. The officer was still clutching a surgical mask to his face, but it could not have helped much with breathing: the air was alarmingly hot and was charged with grey-black smoke. Above the mask Walker saw panic in the man's eyes.

Sir, I want you to turn your car around now and I am going to follow you down. Do it!

And so Walker turned the Volvo around and was grimly escorted off the flaming mountain, leaving behind the cabin he and Maggie had built and all the memories that it harbored. But what made him frantic was the thought that a girl he barely knew and her roan mare were trapped by flames somewhere behind him. As he rolled through the outskirts of town, passing knots of people who stood looking up at the riven landscape above, he told himself that she was camped by the river and that the water would protect her, that she knew the woods well enough not to let herself get pinned down—but the fact was that he needed to know that she was all right, and this knowledge was denied him. As he pulled into the driveway of his home he knew that sleep too would be denied him, perhaps until he knew her fate.

At noon the next day Walker was still sitting at Maggie's old computer in a nook under the stairs, switching back and forth between the local paper's website, the sheriff's site and the national media, scouring every update on the disaster that was playing out a few miles away. In the background the laconic banter of firefighters on the scene spieled on: he had found a website that streamed radio communication between the command center and the fire line, and this had become the backdrop of his night and day. He sensed that by now the work was routine, just hard physical labor; the remaining pockets of homes had been evacuated overnight, many left to burn. Yet this was not the only damage. At a noon press conference the fire chief reported that there were still seven people missing, and this news sent Walker into a new wave of panic. He waited for the names to be given but they were not. Seven not accounted for, and the blaze only thirty percent contained despite the fact that tanker planes had flown dozens of sorties to drop retardant in the path of the flames.

Between forty-five and sixty houses had already been lost and Walker assumed that his was one of them. Though the area was still too dangerous for a proper investigation to commence, early speculation was that the conflagration had begun midway up the east slope of Half-Jack Mountain—very near his cabin—and then gnawed through an enclave of million-dollar homes before roaring down the mountainside toward the creek. It was here that the firemen had chosen to make their stand. Unfortunately Linda's camp had been on the wrong side of the water, directly in the path of the flames. He could only hope that she had raced off on Rona and gotten out of the woods in time.

As the afternoon crawled on, Walker slowly succumbed to exhaustion and finally found himself crying with fatigue. In resignation he collapsed on the sofa with a towel over his burning eyes, falling into a deep and mechanical sleep.

He awoke at seven in the evening with an urgent need to urinate. A bare-knuckled headache had come over him in his sleep, but still he went straight from toilet to computer, desperate for news. At first the updates seemed positive. The wind on the mountain had abated, giving firefighters a chance to close in on the fire, and it was now sixty-five percent contained. He'd read the first paragraph of the article before his eye caught a second article with the headline, One confirmed dead in Half-Jack fire.

Walker devoured the article faster than he had ever read anything in his life. He scanned for her name, but the victim was identified only as a camper who was found by firefighters on the edge of the national forest. There was no mention of the creek, which like much of the area bordered on national forest. The name had not been released, nor the gender, nor the precise cause of death.

Walker rose from his chair and howled in anguish, certain it was her. There was no one to remind him that it might have been anyone; that the woods were full of campers in the summer; that he didn't know whether the lost camper was a woman or a man. Walker went to the kitchen and bent over the butcher-block counter, rolling his hot forehead back and forth across the porous old wood suffused with the scents of Maggie's cooking, of her garlic cloves and carrots and the garden beets she'd cherished, his head filling with the bouquet of her lost life. He spoke her name over and over into the emptiness of the room, wishing she would tell him what to do.

The Half-Jack Fire raged for three days and then lurked in the hills for another week, concealing itself underground and in the trunks of trees only to lash out now and then in sudden anger. At eighteen hours the wind had eased again, giving some hope that the worst was over, but after a brief respite it had come back more rapacious than ever, setting off a new phase of destruction punctuated by exploding propane tanks and the immolation of an antique school bus packed, for reasons known only to its eccentric owner, with Styrofoam. In its long spree the fire consumed fifty-one homes scattered across three valleys, leaving more than two hundred homeless. Five of the destroyed homes belonged to fire-fighters who stayed on the fire line despite being urged to leave. On the summit of Half-Jack Mountain a hotshot crew found two escaped alpacas, their fur singed, huddling in panic as the flames cut off their only route of escape . . .

These were the stories that were leaking out, the legends that were gathering, but at their center was a story far grimmer. It was the story of a young woman and her horse, and it was everywhere in the small town, in every newspaper and on the lips of every café gossip, every neighbor, every television voice. The town harried it as an animal harries a wound.

After hearing of the fire's lone fatality on that second horrible night, Walker knew in his bones that it was Linda. He cried as he had not cried since Maggie's death, talking to himself, lugging his old body from room to room unable to escape the shame of it. Shame, because he was convinced that her death was his fault: in an error of judgment he had sent the firefighters off to his cabin looking for Linda when it was more likely that she was caught somewhere in the dense forest above the creek, desperate to escape the destruction that was charging down the hillside toward her. In his pathetic hubris Walker had convinced himself that she might care enough to come looking for him. Of course she had not, and now she was gone. He tried not to imagine the details of her death but the scene played out in his mind in a hundred terrible variations.

And so he had killed her. But not only in this way, for there was something more. A week after the fire, as he lay exhausted on the living room carpet, two sheriff's deputies and a fire investigator appeared on the front stoop and said they needed to ask him some questions. In a deft fifteen-minute interview they established that it was the poorly doused fire in Walker's pit—the fire he had built for Linda—that had flared back to life and sent out the embers that had ignited Half-Jack Mountain as Walker slept. The investigator laid out the forensic evidence as Walker listened in growing horror. When they asked how he had extinguished his fire he struggled to remember, finally recalling that he had tossed a few handfuls of dirt on the embers and gone back into the house, still intoxicated by Linda's dry lips and her *Not yet*. The puttering coals had not mattered to him while her memory was so fresh; their lurking danger had never entered his consciousness. He told the investigator that he had extinguished the fire with dirt, volunteering no more, his heart paralyzed.

They had gotten what they came for and the consequences would follow. But now there was something he wanted from them.

Please tell me the name of the dead woman, Walker said bluntly.

The three men exchanged querulous looks. It was the fire investigator who spoke first: Do you think you might know something about that fatality?

She was camping down by the creek, just north of the kayak put-in, right? In a red tent?

The investigator watched Walker expressionlessly.

She had a horse. A roan mare. Am I wrong?

Mr. Walker, if you know something about the circumstances of this fatality I suggest you share it now.

Am I right so far?

After a pause the investigator said, Yes, Mr. Walker, you're exactly right so far. What else can you tell us?

I knew her. Slightly. She came that night for peaches and ice cream. We sat around the fire . . .

At this Walker's voice collapsed and he could not go on.

Take your time, Mr. Walker, said the investigator. The two deputies leaned in as if the professor might turn violent. After a false start Walker continued:

Her name was Linda.

At this the investigator leaned back and the two deputies exchanged a look.

Linda what, Mr. Walker?

I have no idea. We'd only just met.

Mr. Walker, what if I told you that her name was not Linda?

Walker frowned at the investigator like a betrayed child. What do you mean? he asked faintly.

Her name was not Linda.

What was it?

It hasn't been released. The family were only notified yesterday.

You need to tell me her name.

The demand hung in the air as the officers conferred quietly.

Mr. Walker, the name will be announced today, so I am going to share it with you and ask that you keep it to yourself until that announcement is made. The name of the deceased was Rona Kirschner.

Rona?

Yes.

Walker smiled mirthlessly and said, She told me Rona was the name of her horse.

I can't comment on that.

And so Walker told the story of Linda, or Rona, such as it was. There really wasn't much to tell beyond an old professor's infatuation with a former student. It was an exhausted old story and it sounded utterly sordid to him in the telling. As they left the house the investigator asked Walker not to leave town until he heard back from them. Walker collapsed onto the sofa, trying to absorb it all, his head pounding erratically, suddenly answerable for the loss of dozens of homes and the life of a young woman he might have loved.

Now Charles Walker is fighting his way through a rainstorm, a deluge that began when he crossed the Idaho-Montana border alongside a livestock trailer loaded with dazed sheep. He is exhausted, and so drives with extra care, taking his eyes off the slick highway only to locate the roll of antacid tablets and the water bottle that have been his companions on the trip. The gnawing in his stomach and the ache at the base of his skull are constant presences now.

Over the past few days Walker has looked within himself and discovered that although homeowners are now being allowed back onto the mountain to check on the fate of their homes, he has no desire to do so. The life he knew on the other side of the conflagration now lies in ashes, whether the cabin still stands or not. Somehow this has freed him to defy the sheriff's request that he not leave town while the investigation is underway, and now he is on the road, a culpable man, perhaps not a monster but certainly a fool.

As his exit nears, the rain suddenly lets up. The open land along the highway is thrown into late afternoon sun, aglow with yellow loosestrife and purple forget-me-nots, but these beauties give Walker no comfort. He pulls off the highway and into the outskirts of the little town, passing a maze of livestock pens, a grain elevator, a shack of a Mexican restaurant. The little houses start, a row of depressing bungalows in drab colors. It has not yet rained here, but the storm is not far behind: he can feel it over his shoulder, tampering with the light, swelling the air. He has outrun it, but not for long.

He pulls over to reread the email from the department secretary, the underlined address, and looks up to see that the street is directly ahead. With the studied care of an honor guard Walker and his tired Volvo slow-march to the light and execute a formal right turn, halting in the middle of the next block.

Not yet, Walker says aloud. She said it only once to him but it has echoed in his mind ever since, a mantra that stubbornly refuses to lead him to enlightenment.

His limbs are heavy and he realizes that he is barely breathing. As he sits in the ragged little town he feels something like death coming over him, but it is not death; death would be a relief, and there is to be no relief. He has never felt so old, so broken and frightened. Yet he has come this far. Walker lifts his foot from the brake and continues down the street, counting off house numbers until he finds the right one. He pulls to the curb just before reaching it, shutting the engine off.

The house is better kept than its neighbors, with a prim lawn, a birdbath, a squat Corinthian column topped by the kind of reflecting globe one might have found in a Henry James garden. The front door is flanked by panels of stained-glass lilies, the stoop by two immaculate boxwoods. In the center of the yard there is even a flagpole, and at the sight of it Walker's gut turns over: the large flag hangs at half mast, furled and still.

He is clutching the handle of the car door, not to open it but to steady himself. *Not yet*, Walker whispers to himself, or perhaps it is Rona whispering to him. He had not expected this, as many times as he's played the moment out in his mind. The sight of the lowered flag is unbearably eloquent. Walker fingers his keys, considering what to do, feeling he might be sick.

After some time a woman appears at the screen door and looks up at the gathering clouds. The scent of rain is on the air now, the light growing strange, for the storm Walker left behind on the highway has followed him at its own lumbering pace. As the woman opens the door and makes her way toward the flagpole, Walker sees that she is much like him: sixty or so, neither attractive nor unattractive, her face careworn, her limbs slow-moving, freighted with grief. Walker's heart closes the distance between them instantly, embracing her, but she notices nothing.

Not yet, says the voice in Walker's head as she carefully lowers the flag, unclips it from its lanyard and folds it with the special diligence accorded a flag that marks a death. She works slowly, with unbroken concentration, tucking in the red and white corners like squared bedsheets until the perfect bundle is done. The first drops of rain are spattering on the Volvo's windshield as Rona's mother gathers the folded flag in her arms and looks up into the storm, studying the clouds and then closing her eyes, rain beginning to darken her pale green dress. Only the quiver of her shoulders reveals how profoundly she is crying.

Now, says Walker, and opens the door without a trace of hesitation, forgetting all the careful words he's prepared.

Head Shy

Angela remembers very little of the abbreviated night she spent with John Renfro, and there's nothing wrong with that kind of forgetting. The night's only traces now are a scent of limestone, a sacrilege, and a missed menstrual period, none of which she's had any trouble keeping to herself. As she sits on the stoop with her friend Louise, she wishes she didn't have to look across the street every day at the bar where she got tangled up with him, but it is what it is; she can't stop going to work just because there is a clear line of sight between the salon and the place where everything went to hell. It doesn't help that her grooming station is closest to the window of the shop, so that as she shampoos toy poodles and trims Bichons and brushes out German shepherds the memory of Renfro is always lurking over her shoulder, a constant reminder of just how stupid a girl can be.

Jesus, Angela, says Louise, picking at her friend's stained violet smock, you're practically wearing that Sheltie.

I hate doing them dogs. They got that undercoat. And I don't think this one had a good brushing its whole life. Mats, tangles, ticks, hot spots everywhere, poor thing.

Louise plucks another strand of butterscotch fur from her friend's shoulder and flicks it into the street. The long summer light is supine now, knocked out on the oil-stained blacktop, hot dust rolling in from the ranches and the remote buttes and tumbling in the air whenever a pickup passes. At the end of the street there is a high hurricane fence, and beyond the fence the tracks of the Union Pacific Overland converging on the switchyard in an arabesque of scalding steel. It has been close to one hundred degrees for five days running and the whole town is exhausted from it.

Talk about a neglected animal, Louise says, pointing with her eyes toward the corner.

Christ, he's the last thing I need to see right now.

It's a she, honey. Cocker spaniel and Golden mix. Sweetest temperament in the world, considering. Only six, seven months old and already busted up like that.

The two women watch John Renfro's wide-eyed puppy labor up the sidewalk with its odd gait, hips seeming to move in a different plane from the rest of the small body, hindquarters executing a corkscrew motion that drives the little torso forward. Yet even from across the street they can see that its expression is open and carefree. The puppy sniffs eagerly at every doorway, on the hunt for something or someone.

Looking for her master, I expect, Louise says as the puppy slaloms toward the open door of the bar. Getting warmer, too.

You think Renfro's in there drinking?

Like as not. Going down the same road as his burnout brother. You know the guy.

Jimmy. Sure. Sits in his beat-to-shit Cherokee sucking on that inhaler all day.

It's lung cancer and it don't stop at the inhaler, I can tell you.

The man starts drinking before he even gets out of bed. Can't hardly breathe, but he sure can drink.

I heard he's slipping away fast now. If you look at him he's just skin and bones, a real cancer face.

Yeah, I seen his brother helping him down out the truck the other day and he was frail as an old lady. On death's door. Got to be hard for John to see that.

Come on, let's get out of this sun and get us an ice cream.

Angela is already halfway to the corner before Louise catches up with her. As they walk away, John Renfro's puppy finds its way to the door of the bar and wobbles inside with its strange drunk walk, for all the world looking like just another regular customer.

———— ════ ————

You sure tore out of there fast, Louise says casually as they sit at the sticky picnic table with their ice cream cones.

Angela hesitates, stopped by a thick wave of nausea as the mint chocolate coats her stomach.

You don't look so good, Angie.

I don't feel so good. Been puking for a couple days now.

Louise regards her friend with grey eyes gone suddenly gentle. Angie, you didn't go and get yourself knocked up, did you?

By way of reply Angela bends over and vomits the gluey green remains of her ice cream onto the curb. At the same moment a blaring electronic horn announces the approach of one of the freight trains hauling yellowcake down from the uranium mines up north. The unforgiving bark of it ricochets down the street, banking off the old buildings like a scuttling hand grenade. The sound covers Angela's retching, but only just.

Oh Jesus! says Louise, pulling a wad of napkins from the dispenser and throwing an arm around her friend. You're really sick. Go on inside and get cleaned up—I'll take care of this. You want me to come with you?

A few minutes later Angela returns to the table, ashen and exhausted, her gaze shuttered. There is a deep trundling vibration in the ground as the long freight train crawls through the rail yard and is switched south at the semaphore tree.

What is it? asks Louise over the low and unstoppable rumble. I'm such a fuck-up. Sorry.

What are you talking about, gorgeous? Under the table Louise lays a hand on Angela's knee and discovers that it is in motion, jittering up and down furiously.

Jesus, Angie, what the hell is wrong with you?

Louise, I wasn't going to tell nobody this, but I made it with John Renfro.

For a long moment Louise regards her friend with an astonishment that gives way to distaste. He's a loser, she says at last. You shouldn't of. How the hell did you let that happen?

Angela is in tears now. He drank me blind, she says. I browned out, is all. I browned out and went upstairs with him.

Louise lets out a low whistle.

And not only that, Angela continues. I played my V card for that asshole.

Louise smiles darkly, truly surprised now. You're a virgin, honey? But I thought you and Tommy Driggs—

Was is the word you want. I *was* one. Tommy didn't ever get what he came looking for. He got other things, but not that.

This is way bad.

It gets worse, Louise.

I'm right there with you, sister. I get it. You let that loser knock you up. And now what.

The friends fall silent for a long moment, the train filling the sweltering silence like a prairie thunderstorm. A pair of gossiping young girls, fourteen or fifteen years old, pass the table on their way to get ice cream cones at The Cold Plunge, leaving a smell of cheap lemon cologne in the air.

Look at us there, says Louise, squeezing Angela's knee. That was us not so long ago.

What am I gonna do, Louise? says Angela, her face a blur of muddied mascara.

You're going to keep out of that asshole's way, Angie. We got to work this on our own. Don't go crying to John Renfro, all right?

It's his baby, Louise.

But it's your ass on the line, ain't it. Don't underestimate the meanness in that man. This is news he don't want to hear. You got to keep it quiet. Keep it between us.

Angela cries silently, face lowered into her folded arms, as the ore train rumbles off into the late afternoon. After a long while Louise says gently, You know why Renfro's dog gimps around like it does, don't you, Angie?

Mm, says Angela.

You ever try to pet that puppy? It's head shy, Angie, real fearful. It's got a sweet disposition, but you bring your hand anywhere near that puppy's head it'll shy right away from you. Renfro's kicked the crap out of that poor animal. I know the litter it came from and not one of those other puppies has a hip issue. Renfro did that. You can take that to the bank. And that's why you got to keep this to yourself. You can't go to him with this.

I know, Angela says in a voice so quiet Louise can barely follow it. You're right.

After a while Angela raises her head and rests her chin in her hands, gazing wanly at her friend across the picnic table etched with the names of lovers she knows. Her eyes are weary but clear, washed out by the heavy heat and by her crying. She reaches across and touches the small stars tattooed on her friend's long neck, considering them, and a memory comes to her.

You know what he told me?

Do I really want to know?

He said that when he got engaged to his ex he couldn't afford to give her a real ring, so instead he bought her a tattoo of one. Said at least she'd never lose it. Right there.

Angela points to her friend's ring finger, tracing the imagined tattoo with her fingertip.

And you know what? He was proud of that. Louise, he was proud of it.

I'll bet she ain't, says Louise.

Renfro had introduced her to a drink called the tequila boilermaker on the night she slept with him, in a booth with a slashed seat at the back of Riley's On First, and after drinking two of them she'd gotten up and roundhoused unsteadily over to his side of the table. Not to sit, exactly, but rather to slump with her head in his lap close to where his penis lay hidden and restive: she felt the denim hunker up and then his long fingers insinuating themselves into the curls of her fallen perm, his palm cupping the back of her head to guide it. When the waitress came by he ordered another round coolly and managed to light a cigarette with his free hand, flicking the lighter open and snapping it closed again like the bolt of a tiny rifle. In her drunkenness this charmed her and to reward him she took the raised denim hump of his erection between her teeth and gently teased him, feeling him respond instantly. My kind of girl, he laughed, and pulled her head down hard.

None of this would she remember later, nor would she recall how it was that she found herself alone with him in the stifling storage room above the bar. There was a perforated mattress on the floor among the beer crates and cleaning supplies and broken red vinyl bar stools and that is where Renfro led her, shinnying her jeans and panties off in a matter of seconds. If she protested, she would not remember it later: what she recalled instead was the smell of quarry rock about him as he bore down on her. Everything about him, from his clothes to his lips to the sparse hair on his chest, smelled of limestone, as if she were pressing her face not against a man but against the cool wall of the old bank building on Third Street, or perhaps, she thought, against a gravestone.

Of all that happened or might have happened on the filthy mattress that night, the only other thing she recalled clearly was the moment when he rolled off her to loot a longneck beer out of an open case and with dazed surprise she saw, of all things, a Bible lying on the floor within easy reach. It was a Jimmy Swaggart and she noticed that it was the Giant Print edition—the very same one her own mother had kept at her bedside since Angela was a teenager.

It made no sense. Did some dried-out, snake-handling tongue-speaker come up there on slow afternoons to lie down on the stained mattress and read Revelation? It felt deeply out of place, and when Renfro finished off the beer and thumped the bottle down atop the Jimmy Swaggart as if it were a fat coaster she felt a twinge of wrongness, a pang of sacrilege, despite being as drunk as she'd ever been in her twenty-three years. The beer bottle sat there on the Good News sweating like a wrangler in the noon-day sun, a terrible thing. Though she hadn't seen the inside of a church since leaving her parents' home she reached over and moved the bottle to the floor as John Renfro mounted her for another ride. Somewhere in the blurry and endless midsection of the following day she would remember that small decision she'd made, that small and instinctive gesture of rectitude, and would feel that it was the best thing she'd done in a long time.

Renfro smelled of limestone dust that night despite the fact that it was his day off—that was how deeply ingrained it was in him, and how little effort he made to shake it off when the work was done. Since the beginning of the summer he had taken the night shift by choice, riding his dirt bike down the I-80 frontage road past the stupendous wind farms and the broken cinnamon-colored buttes disappearing into the dusk and the white limestone slashes on his left that reflected the failing light for a few minutes longer than the red sandstone on his right. The ride took forty minutes and it gave him time to stretch out, to clear his head before the night of hypnotic work, before he descended into the pit under the gigantic halogen spotlights and mounted the back-hoe or the grader or the vertical conveyor, whichever machine the foreman pointed him to. He prided himself on being the only guy in the whole operation who could rotate through every rig with ease. He would work under the piercing lights until his two o'clock lunch break and then hike up out of the pit and down into a ravaged arroyo to eat his sandwich, half-blinded by the hours of dust and artificial glare, unable to see the stars until a few minutes before it was time to go back down into the blazing pit and finish out the night.

Sometimes he would think of the land while riding his bike back home, the deadpan hills that had been home to the Coman-che, then to the marauding Sioux and now to the beaten-down Shoshone and Arapaho scattered along the Wind River Range, but most nights he would think of women and what they had done to him. As the land gaped toward the horizon on both sides of the highway he would tell himself that his ex, for one, deserved every card he'd dealt her, up to and including the moment when she'd asked him for the divorce and he'd knocked her lights out in the bathroom. He was dead sure she was sleeping around behind his back, but couldn't prove it despite lurking outside the steak house to see who met her after her shift (only her girlfriend Annie) and trailing her to what she claimed was church (it was). In his gut he knew she was a liar and he was glad to put her behind him even if it had cost him the Pontiac and the shithole house. In the weeks after the marriage came apart he said these things to himself over and over again during his nighttime rides along I-80, sometimes shouting over the road noise so that he could hear himself think.

He went back to sleeping with the local girls, including one fifteen-year-old whose lean hips and pierced privates could have landed him in jail for a long time. And he got the dog, just to take it off his older brother's hands when he saw that his brother was too sick and too drunk to remember to feed it. The cancer that had started in Jimmy's lungs had gone to his brain and was on a tear now, unstoppable as the August heat; every day Jimmy acted crazier, a danger to himself and a vision of pure pain to his younger brother. It was only a matter of time before he would set his apartment on fire somehow or walk into traffic or drink himself into a coma, though the cancer would probably take him first. He'd stopped all the treatments now and his weight was well south of a hundred pounds. Sometimes his cough, alternately gurgling and hacking, would go on for the better part of an hour, a terrifying thing to John Renfro who from time to time caught himself coughing up limestone dust.

And so Renfro had stolen the puppy one day in order to save it. He had meant to palm the animal off on the next girl he slept with—it was a puppy any girl would fall in love with—but the thing followed him around with such eager loyalty that he soon found he did not want to get rid of it. He taught it to come when he whistled his wolf whistle and this pleased him. He didn't bother to name it until it crapped in the trailer's kitchenette and he sent it flying with his steel-toed boot, at which point the name Roadkill came to him and he stayed up half the night laughing and shouting the name at the terrified puppy as it nestled, shaking uncontrollably, in a pile of his dirty clothes. The puppy never walked right after that kick, but in a few days it began to limp around after him almost as if nothing had ever happened. If he went to touch the puppy it would rear back and shy away, but apart from that it seemed to have forgiven him entirely.

You're a real dumb fuck, ain't you? Renfro asked the puppy, shaking his head in disbelief. A dude beats tar out of you and you follow him around asking for another licking. That's what I call shit-stupid. No other word for it.

He kept the puppy around—girls came and went forgettably, but he kept the puppy around and even built it a special crate with a quilted blue mover's blanket where it could rest its ruined hips when he went off to work. He fed it hamburger and bacon and lunch meat, and when despite all this the puppy refused to be pet he would switch on the little orange amplifier and hammer out death metal on his electric guitar in the stifling confines of the trailer, trying not to think too hard about the whys and wherefores of it.

Goddamn it, Angela says to Louise, I left my stuff at work. I got my cigarettes and three Powerball tickets in my bag. I'm just not thinking straight. Come with me?

The two women leave the ice cream shop and begin strolling back toward the salon, passing the resale place and the auto parts store and the shuttered Christmas shop, dormant until Thanksgiving. The worst heat of the day is over now and the sky is settling down into a golden light, high clouds just beginning to mass for the sunset to come.

Across the tracks there lies a small neighborhood of run-down houses, mostly Arapaho, then the bus station and an abandoned lot festering with high weeds, and then, without warning, the open land rolling out toward the distant buttes that don't look entirely real until this time of day. At the close of a summer afternoon the sun picks them out and what had seemed no more than a pale red mirage is suddenly revealed as a procession of hotly glowing monuments. As the two friends round the corner onto First, this illumination is at its peak, magnetizing the life of the town toward the west.

Hey, check it out, says Angela when they're nearly at the salon. Look at Don Wop trying to hook in the tourists.

On the broad sidewalk outside Riley's On First stands Don Ciccarelli, the bartender, at this moment gesturing expansively to a short fat man in fake cowboy attire and his stout wife in pink Spandex shorts and flipflops. The man's black Stetson is too big, but it seems no one has disclosed this to him.

He's telling about the bullet hole in the mirror, says Louise sourly.

Yeah, I know, Angela says, quoting from memory: I invite you to step inside and see the famous hole made by a jilted cowboy in anger. It was a six-shooter that made that bullet hole. You're welcome to come on in, no obligation to have a drink. People come from all over the *world* to see our famous mirror. The owner refuses to have it repaired out of a sense of history. Come on in and photograph it if you like. On the house.

What a steaming pile of shit, says Louise.

They linger for a few moments inside the grooming salon, still somewhat cool from the day's air conditioning, Louise leaning against her work table to file a long, glitter-dusted nail. So Angie, she says after a time, what do you reckon you're going to do about the baby? There's places in Cheyenne you can get it done if you want to.

I don't know, Angela replies in a confidential tone, though there is no one else in the shop. I don't know what to do.

How far along are you, you think?

Not much. Only missed the one period is all.

If you need money for it I'd be good for that.

And all at once Angela is sobbing again, slumped in one of the customer chairs, a wreck of tears.

If I get rid of it I want that asshole to pay. He took advantage.

If you get rid of it? There ain't no *if* about it, Angie. You can't afford to have a baby, least of all the baby of a man like that. I'll go with you. And like I said, I'll lend you the money. You don't got to go to him.

It ain't about the money, Louise. It's about him doing the right thing by a girl he fucked and forgot. You know what I mean?

Angie, the guy's a wildcard even when his brother isn't about to drop dead of cancer. Keep your distance. He don't need to hear this now.

Let's get out of here. I need a smoke.

Louise and Angela lock the shop up behind them and turn to

see the bartender Ciccarelli crossing the street toward them, Renfro's dog laboring at his heels. Ciccarelli's left eye was knocked off its orbit years ago by a stray punch, and now he seems to regard the two women separately, Angela through the left eye and Louise through the right.

So, Don, says Louise, you get some more tourists yanked in there to see the big bad bullet hole?

These particular individuals were from the Ukraine and they were quite intrigued, Ciccarelli replies, hands in his pockets, his stray eye looking rheumy in the heat. In Ukraine they seem to have had quite a lot of experience with bullets and the like. It's something our two regions have in common. The man correctly guessed the caliber by looking at the hole.

Louise laughs. Chickie, you're the well-spokenest bartender in America.

The puppy catches up to Ciccarelli just as he steps up onto the sidewalk with his polished boots, but it can't make the short hop to clear the curb. Instead it plants its front paws next to Ciccarelli's feet and through a convoluted maneuver drags its hips up behind it. The sight of this small struggle brings Angela to her knees and she takes the dog in her arms, crying over it, its hips swiveling wildly in an attempt to get free. With an anxious whimpering the puppy pleads to be left alone.

That dog clearly prefers not to be handled, says Ciccarelli.

Yeah, Angie, you best set her down before she gets snappish.

But Angela will not let go. She holds the small golden body to her breast so firmly that it has no choice but to quiet down, and after a long moment the puppy rests its chin on her shoulder, panting fast, exhausted. Angela closes her eyes, rocking it gently. The puppy's eyes go unfocused and calm.

Damn if you didn't do it, says Louise, impressed.

I don't think that puppy has ever let itself be held, says Ciccarelli. You must really know your dogs. But of course you do.

For a suspended moment the three of them stand without speaking further, the sun passing behind the salon and throwing them into welcome shadow. The puppy seems to doze, sighing quietly. Along First Street the restaurants are starting to open for the dinner hour and the scent of steak flows past like music.

It is then that Louise sees John Renfro explode from the door of Riley's On First, a beer bottle in his hand and fury plainly visible in his face even from across the street.

Angie, let's go get us a pizza, she says, watching Renfro over Angela's shoulder. Her friend's eyes are closed as she sways gently with the puppy, in her own world.

Not hungry, says Angela quietly. My stomach's still off.

Across the street, Renfro draws a cell phone from his jeans pocket and dials a number, scraping his fingers through his unwashed hair as it rings. He begins to pace haphazardly, crisscrossing the sidewalk in front of Riley's. When the call is answered he stops suddenly and within seconds is cursing into the tiny phone, setting his beer down so he can hammer at the swollen air with a sharp fist. Anyone can see that there is a lot of liquor in him.

When Renfro disconnects he falls against the warm brick wall of the building and sinks into a crouch, talking fervidly to himself. Watching this, Louise wonders for an instant whether there was anyone at all on the other end of the phone, so self-contained is his distress. But she has no time to consider it further. As if through a silent shout, Renfro and Angela have each become aware of the other's presence. Angela opens her eyes in alarm, having perhaps realized whose voice has been brawling its way across First Street, and at just this moment Renfro spots her cradling his puppy not thirty feet away. Hey! he shouts hoarsely. What the fuck you doing with my dog?

Angela turns to see the roaring man wedging his way between two parked pickups, coming straight for her.

We gotta go, Angie, says Louise quickly. Let's get out of here.

But Ciccarelli calls out to Renfro: You ought to be grateful that these ladies are minding your puppy, John. Maybe they'll take her to the vet like you should have done after you kicked her half to death.

At this Renfro plants a palm on the hood of a red Impala that is waiting for the light to change and hurtles over it. He comes after Ciccarelli like a man afire.

Ciccarelli braces himself, unclipping a ring of keys from his belt and deftly arranging them so that a sharp key shaft juts from between each pair of fingers, but in the last instant Angela steps between the two men, Renfro's puppy still placid in her arms.

Angie! cries Louise. What you doing?

The liquor in Renfro suddenly takes him down. Whatever purity of hatred had enabled him to fly across the road like a sprinter is now played out, and he stumbles gracelessly over the curb, sprawling to the sidewalk. Ciccarelli takes advantage of the moment to disappear into the entryway of the Chinese restaurant two doors down.

Shit! says Renfro, trying to get to his feet but badly off balance.

At this Angela delivers a sharp kick to his lower belly and he falls back onto the cement, utterly startled. She follows with a kick to his crotch, but misses when he rolls away.

Put my fucking dog down, he says thickly. Leave her be.

You don't deserve this dog, John.

A puzzled look crosses Renfro's face, as if he is surprised that she knows his name.

Already forgotten me, you asshole?

Renfro regards her mutely.

Because you shouldn't forget the mother of your child, John. You shouldn't never forget.

What the fuck are you talking about? Put my dog down.

You knocked me up is what I'm talking about. Or don't you recall our dreamy night together?

Renfro has managed to get to his feet, but as the news sinks in he bends over to rest his hands on his knees like an old man gone suddenly dizzy. He says nothing at all, just hovering there in his standing crouch, utterly defeated. It is so unexpected, so strange, that Angela and Louise exchange a look of concern.

Renfro? ventures Louise.

They wait. You all right, Renfro? she tries again.

When at last John Renfro straightens and looks up at them his face is streaming with tears. It strikes both women that he looks unwell, drawn and pale and unwashed in a way that wasn't obvious in the fury of a moment before.

Shit, John, you don't look so good, says Louise. Almost as tore up as your brother.

At this Renfro swallows hard and coughs on his own saliva. He seems to have trouble catching a breath.

Jesus, Renfro, I'm sorry I said that. That was an awful thing to say.

But now Renfro is looking at Angela. She stands over him defiantly, the puppy somehow still placid in her arms, hypnotized by the simple contact of her body. Renfro, she says, you know you got to pay for the abortion. There's no discussing it.

The words seem to pass through him like the sound of rain or river rapids rather than of language. His shoulders are hunched, drawing his muscular arms in protectively. Renfro looks away for a long moment, then looks at the puppy curled over her shoulder and finally at her.

Give me back my dog, he says under his breath.

There is no threat in his voice. It is the simplest of requests.

Angie, says Louise.

Give me two hundred dollars so I can do what I need to do and I'll give you the dog back, says Angela. Maybe I will.

Angie! whispers Louise loudly.

I don't got it. I don't got two hundred dollars.

Do you even remember my name?

Renfro lets out a long sigh, falling back against the brick wall of the salon. Still he seems short of breath. A new runnel of tears starts down his hard cheek and he makes no effort to conceal it. Why you ask me that, he says.

As if scenting the strangeness in the air, the puppy rouses from its trance and begins to squirm in Angela's arms, wanting to free itself. Angela coos to it but the puppy isn't listening: it needs to be back on solid ground. After a gentle struggle Angela relents and lowers it carefully to the sidewalk.

The puppy stands still for a moment, getting its bearings. When Angela bends down to stroke its flank it falls back on its haunches awkwardly, submitting to her affections, until her hand strays toward its butterscotch head. Abruptly the puppy ducks away, losing its balance and falling sideways onto the cement. As it works to right itself the ground below quivers slightly, almost imperceptibly, signaling the plodding approach of another ore train, and the tiny movement seems to urge the puppy to its unsteady feet.

Renfro sends out a low wolf whistle and the puppy turns toward him out of habit, for this is part of the meager language they've shared in their short time together. When Renfro starts to walk away, seeming to sober up with every step, the puppy is set in motion like a broken toy, hobbling away behind its master without a glance back at the woman who was for a short moment its protector. Louise threads an arm through her friend's, squeezing it gently, as Angela watches Renfro and his trusting puppy wander off toward the tracks.

Once Renfro is out of sight, Ciccarelli emerges from his hiding place in the entryway of the Chinese place.

What do you want? says Louise.

I heard it all. Couldn't see real well, but I heard everything. And I've got to tell you two ladies something. It's something you should know.

They ignore him for a long moment, but slowly they come around.

Go ahead, says Angela.

That thing about you being pregnant with Renfro's kid—that wasn't the only bad news he's had today. It's why he reacted the way he did. You know, caving in like that. More bad news than a man could handle, I guess.

What are you talking about?

Ciccarelli scans the street with his weird, wall-eyed gaze and says:

John Renfro's been sitting at the bar for the last two hours telling the whole world about his diagnosis. Not like anyone wanted to hear it, but he had to tell it.

What diagnosis?

This morning he got the news that he's got exactly what's killing his brother Jimmy. Cancer of the lung.

But he ain't a smoker, protests Angela.

He works with all that dust down in the quarry, doesn't he? Or who knows, it could just be hereditary—there's his big brother, and their daddy died of cancer too. Morgan Renfro always had a chaw in his cheek but as far as I know he never smoked a cigarette in his life. Ever hear of nonsmoker's lung cancer? Can happen to anyone.

The two friends are speechless, the slowly gathering sound of the freight leaving no room for words.

So, concludes Ciccarelli, now you've got some understanding of why he reacted like he did. Renfro's a rattlesnake but this just laid him out.

Come on, Angela says to Louise, come with me. Without another word to Ciccarelli the two women start walking down toward the end of the street.

Up ahead, Renfro and the puppy are making their way up the sloping ramp that leads to a high trestle from which one can view the trains passing below. It is a favorite spot from which to take in the gradual unfolding of the sunset and they can see pairs of lovers and smoking teenagers and married couples already leaning on the railing up above. The Ukrainian tourists are there too, the wife fiddling with her camera, changing batteries, getting ready.

Renfro makes his way up the ramp quickly for a man with so much drink in him, the puppy struggling to keep up, driving itself upslope against gravity with its corkscrew gait. By the time Louise and Angela reach the base of the ramp Renfro is hoisting the puppy over the tall step at the top.

Let's go up, says Angela.

Shit no.

Why not?

You don't want to be seen. That guy's half crazy. Why would you want to get anywhere near him?

Angela considers this carefully. I think, she says, I smell trouble.

Renfro and his puppy are walking across the trestle now, passing behind the others. The ore train growls in from the west as if charging out of the late sun's glare, as much a part of the town as the frontier-era pavers on Third Street, the smell of wheat chaff hovering around the mills, the sprawling sunset over the buttes. Tourists adore it, this stampeding rumble of heavy wheels and uranium ore and flaming orange crew cars.

Up on the overlook bridge the Ukrainian woman is aiming her pocket camera at the oncoming train, photographing it first horizontally, then vertically, then horizontally again. She will show the pictures to her friends back in Kiev or Sebastopol and bore them with every detail of the visit, starting with the bullet hole in the saloon mirror and culminating in this vision of a massive ore train crawling toward her from the maw of a beatific American sunset, a high plains sundown from an old movie. She cannot stop taking pictures. Her husband in his absurd cowboy getup, meanwhile, leans over the guard rail, smoking dismissively, his red face nearly obscured by a pair of outsize sunglasses.

Angela and Louise watch from below as Renfro approaches the Ukrainians and exchanges a few words with the husband. The Ukrainian half turns, leaning back on the rail, and offers Renfro a cigarette: they watch Renfro refuse it and then change his mind, accepting a light from the other man.

Goddamn if he isn't lighting up, says Louise in astonishment. Just diagnosed with lung cancer and he's celebrating with a smoke.

Angela starts walking toward the ramp that leads up to the trestle.

Angie! says Louise, raising her voice to overcome the sound of the train. Hold up!

But Angela is already moving up the incline. It is only as she reaches the top of the ramp that Louise catches up with her and locks her arm in a firm grip to stop her from going farther.

You stay right here, girl.

Let me go, Louise. I don't like the way this is shaping up.

But Louise will not relinquish her grip. From the edge of the footbridge the two women see Renfro give a little cowboy salute to the tourist, a bit of undetected mockery. As the train passes the first signal, he throws a long leg over the railing and swivels around so that he is poised like a kid in a tree, unable to grasp the handrail because he is now bearing the squirming puppy in his arms.

Angela and Louise scream at the same instant. It is too loud now to hear what anyone is saying but everyone sees the dangling man watch the train come on, the puppy panicking in his arms and making him shift his weight so that he won't fall. Renfro rocks and bucks atop the narrow railing like a dirt biker hitting rough terrain, the alcohol working against him. Meanwhile the ore train is switched to the left track and takes to the new rails with a metallic jerk.

Jesus Christ, Louise, let me go! says Angela, clawing at her friend's grip with tears in her eyes. I got to stop him doing whatever the hell he's going to do!

No, you don't got to, Angie.

I got to stop this! At least for the puppy.

You can't. Forget it. It's out of our hands.

And so they watch as the train passes the last signal and hammers toward the overpass. Renfro readies himself, leaning forward with the terrified puppy in his arms and closing his eyes, his drawn face unreadable in the sun's glare. A dozen people watch in shock, church women and dude ranch vacationers and the county prosecutor and a pair of high school boys with greased-up hair, not one of them able to move or even speak. It is all happening too quickly, too strangely, the roar of the train bearing down with its incalculable weight and power.

Only the Ukrainian woman escapes the sudden paralysis. She leans over the railing next to Renfro, stretching out her chunky arms and shouting to him above the train's growl, pleading with him. It seems for a brief moment that Renfro is listening, opening his eyes and leaning slightly toward her as if to make out her words.

No one will ever know what the Ukrainian woman says to him, but only that it changes Renfro at the last possible instant. As the train consumes the final twenty feet of track Renfro suddenly hands the terrified puppy over into her waiting arms, twisting back awkwardly as if to spare her from having to lean over the rail. The puppy kicks once as it leaves his grasp, launching itself from Renfro's chest—or perhaps it is Renfro who launches himself by pushing back against the fleeing puppy's momentum, letting the sharp wriggle and kick throw him off balance. Whatever the case, as his puppy sprawls across the Ukrainian woman's ample chest Renfro slips off the railing like a man sliding casually off a bar stool, unsteady but not much troubled by it. They all see his arms flap loose as he falls into the path of the train, and those who can't avert their eyes watch in horror as his lean torso is bundled under the engine and rendered into a long crimson slick that the fire department later will blast away with hoses and finally with the thick foam they lay onto wildfires, as if the heat of Renfro's passing cannot be quelled in any other way.

A week after Renfro's death Louise flicks her blinker on and turns right at the last light in town, pointing her pickup toward open country.

Where you going? asks Angela, almost doubled over on the bench seat, clutching her knees to her chest. I need to get home is all.

Just a quick stop. How much pain you in?

It hurts like hell, Louise. More than they said it would. Like ten times the worst cramps you ever had.

Louise reaches across her friend and fusses in the glove compartment until she comes up with a pill bottle.

Take one of these, she says.

What is it?

Some of that nice candy they gave me for my back. You'll be feeling no pain before you know what hit you. You still got some Coke to wash it down with?

As Angela swallows the pill Louise pulls the truck onto a rutted two-track that leads down to an impeccable little house. There is pasture all around but no sign of stock. As the truck jerks through the ruts Angela groans, every jolt an assault.

They pull in to a short gravel drive that leads to the front door of the house. You wait here, says Louise, leaning over her friend to roll the passenger window down and then closing the truck door gently behind her. Even in her pain Angela is surprised when the bartender Ciccarelli answers Louise's ring and opens the screen door to usher her in.

Angela closes her eyes and tries relaxing her grip on her knees, praying that the drug will kick in quickly. She is studying her own insides like a woman diving blind through an undersea cave, feeling for danger in the impenetrable darkness. The whole day had started off wrong when she woke up with a migraine—as if any day could start right when its central event was driving an hour in a pickup with broken air conditioning only to be rewarded with an abortion. But the doctor had been kind, a serious woman who was raised on a cutting-horse ranch nearby and seemed to understand, without asking, how a woman like Angela could wind up carrying the baby of a dead man. Only the sound of the fatal vacuum and now these vise-like cramps had made it terrible, and nothing the lady doctor could say would have changed that. All this Angela goes over again and again in her mind as she waits in the hot truck, wondering what the hell is taking Louise so long. Is she in bed with Ciccarelli, balling the wall-eyed Italian while her best friend stews in the heat with her insides torn up?

Angela may be imagining it, but the pain pill already seems to be taking effect. As she sits rehearsing the sharp words she will say to Louise upon her return, the cramps begin to dull slightly and a lulling mood slips over her, a kind of slow seduction: there are magpies and whiskeyjacks in the pasture that she only now hears, and this almost makes her smile. A lightness floods through her thighs and then a knot of pain relaxes in her gut, freeing something in her; after a moment her head lolls back on the headrest and for the first time in hours she stops thinking about what's happened. She closes her eyes, faintly aware of the sounds of the late afternoon, of the scent of rye. In the distance a screen door slaps shut, a hummingbird drills past, voices burble.

It is stifling in the truck and instinctively Angela lazes toward the window, needing air. It is here that her cheek comes to rest against something soft and very much alive. When she opens her eyes Renfro's puppy is only inches from her face, looking at her with a curiosity that seems nearly human. Oh, she says drowsily, aware of its light breath on her cheek. With this the puppy seems to reach a decision and begins to lick her face, starting at the sharp line of her jaw.

Shit! Stop it! Angela says furiously, and with a jerk of her head shies away from the little tongue.

Louise leans into the truck over the window sill, the puppy wriggling in her arms. Angie, she says, be cool. Look who come to see you.

Get that fucking animal out of my face, Louise.

She just wants to be friends. She don't mean nothing more by it.

I don't need no friends like that, Angela says, wiping at the invisible trail of the puppy's saliva with the back of her hand.

But Angela, says Ciccarelli calmly, that puppy came looking for you. And now just listen to your attitude.

Angela looks past her friend at the bartender, his face reduced to a pair of eyes that don't quite line up.

Came looking for me how?

You remember how Renfro handed his pup over to that Ukrainian lady right before he jumped?

Fell, says Angie evenly.

All right, fell. Whatever the case, in all the confusion this puppy disappeared—the woman must have dropped her, or set her down. After what happened to Renfro I guess no one paid any mind.

So what?

So, two days later I'm standing outside the bar and I see this very puppy across the street, outside the salon, looking for you.

Not looking for me.

Obviously looking for you.

For sure, agrees Louise. Angie, remember how she'd go looking for Renfro in the bar? So now she sits by the door of the salon and won't budge. She's looking for you.

Don't talk shit, says Angela, studying the accelerator pedal. After a considerable pause she says more quietly, I know why you're doin' this but it ain't going to work.

We're asking you to take her, says Ciccarelli. I'm allergic. I can't keep this animal.

So give it to the shelter.

Louise shakes her head. No one going to adopt a puppy with hips like that and you know it. They'll put her down after three days, like they do.

So you keep her.

I can't, Angie. You know my lease don't let me have pets.

That puppy's stone bad luck and you know it. Wasn't for that puppy, John Renfro might still be around.

It wasn't the puppy's fault what happened to that loser! protests Louise.

You don't know that. You saw it kick Renfro back off that railing.

Angie, she's just a puppy—even if that happened, and I ain't saying that's what happened, you can't blame the animal.

I don't want no connection to that man.

All right, Angie, but will you just take her for a minute here. I got to set her down.

Without waiting for an answer, Louise passes the puppy through the truck window and sets it gently on her friend's lap.

No, says Angela angrily, no fucking way. I can't. Get it away from me!

Angela tries to lean back to escape the puppy, but the seat is hard up against the rear window of the truck cab and there is nowhere to go. The small golden body stretches out along Angela's closed thighs, its head nestling where they meet.

Look what she's sniffing at, says Louise, trying to smile as the puppy burrows lightly between Angela's legs.

As if embarrassed, the little animal wriggles and shifts itself higher, resting its head against Angela's belly, its troubled hips akimbo between her knees. But before it can settle in comfortably Angela flings open the driver's side door and shoves the dog to the floor, sliding her hips past the steering wheel. The puppy scrambles out the open door behind her and shelters behind a balding tire, panting hard.

Angela is gone, half running and half stumbling into the immaculate pasture before Louise or Ciccarelli can react. By the time they come around the pickup she has reached the exact center of the field. Her arrival flushes a pair of magpies from the pristine rye and they loft heavily into the thick dusk, complaining in full-throated anger.

Angie! calls Louise, stepping through the high grass.

Stay away, says Angela.

Come on, Angie, I didn't mean nothing by it. I'm sorry.

Stay the fuck away from me, Louise!

At this Louise stops making her way through the field, still a good thirty feet from Angela, for all at once there is a vein of panic in her friend's voice. Okay, she says in the calmest tone she can muster, okay. I'll wait right here.

Angela stands where she is for a long while, arms wrapped around herself in the gathering darkness. From time to time she says a few words under her breath, or looks up at the heavens, or shifts her weight from one leg to the other, but she doesn't move from her spot at the center of the field. At some point she has a good cry, the sound of her suffering stumbling out across the pastureland. Louise and Ciccarelli listen but keep their distance, not daring to approach her. The darkness pulls in closer as the crickets and cicadas come on, and then the distant creek frogs, thousands of primitive conversations burgeoning in the moonless night.

Eventually Angela sits down cross-legged in the dark of the pasture and begins tearing at the high grasses as if clearing ground for a nest. Her crying has died away, fading to a silence that is utterly private, utterly inviolable. In the dark pasture there are no words now; there is no persuasion or complaint. The night has moved past words into a mute stalemate, the three of them bound in place by the suffering of one.

Eventually Ciccarelli and Louise walk back to the house and climb the three steps to the porch. Ciccarelli flicks a light on and they can see Angela out in the field, her ghostly head and shoulders hovering above the tall rye grass like a strange marine creature drifting on calm seas. They sit on Ciccarelli's slatted porch bench and watch her without knowing what to say, the night wearing on, until the bartender covers Louise's hand with his and after some time leads her into the house, the screen door snapping quietly behind them. And so by the time midnight comes they are alone, Angela and the puppy, sitting two feet apart in silent colloquy in the hidden nest that Angela's grief has made.

Boy, Unleashed

I told the man Myra didn't have no say in it. There wasn't no other way to keep the boy from running off, so I took and put him on that lead like I done plenty of times before. A man's got to tend to the safety of his child when he lives in the back hills.

It wasn't no harm to him—it's a good long lead, take him almost to the fence line if he want to, because with his condition he needs to run all the time. You'll never find a Ozark copperhead high-spirited as that boy. The Lord only knows what he'd grow up to be if growing up was in the cards for him, which it plainly ain't.

But then the man come around and arrest Myra and try and take the boy away. I'm having a smoke out back and I don't even see them drive up. But when I hear Myra, I know something's going south fast. She's a large woman and she got the lungs of a negro preacher when she lose her temper. I'm hearing some real language out front the house, and I can hear it in her voice she's half in the bag again. I can tell you, the boy and me both know to get out her way when she goes off like that.

When I come back round the house there's this tall negro in a necktie there with two deputies, and they already got Myra under arrest. The negro's a fair copy of that negro president they put in. There's a latin lady there too, but not much to look at. She's kneeled down talking to my boy, askin' him what-all. She's a Child Services lady, but not like that Bonnie Scott, the one that usually comes round. Bonnie's good people. I knew her daddy in the service. Well I can see by the boy's face he's scared half to death of this new gal. He don't want no strangers hauling his momma off to a Fayetteville jail cell. It's a bad day for him, and I don't care what they say. They the cause of the trouble, not Myra and me. We got nothing but love and consideration for our boy. The Good Lord knows we give up a lot for him with his mental condition. You can't imagine the half of it.

"I leashed Bobby up," I tell the negro. "It ain't Myra you want."

He puts his hand up to stop me talking because he's busy talking to John Law about whatnot. He takes his time. They already got Myra locked in the back of the cruiser—I can see her through the window. I can hear her wedding band banging on the glass and I think what a thing it would be if that little band could bust her out.

Finally the man says, "Do you have something to tell us? About the leash and the bruises?"

"I'm the one leashed the boy up. I'm the one you should put in that cruiser."

"How did your son come by those welts on his face?"

"I don't know nothing about that. I been working in the smokehouse all morning."

"We've got a file here, Mr. Jackson," he says.

"Myra was wrongly accused before, and you're fixing to wrongly accuse her now."

"Are you saying that you tied the boy up but you have no knowledge of who struck him? Is that your statement to me?"

"You got to understand the boy's condition."

"I am well aware. But we don't make a mentally challenged boy wear a dog collar and chain him up in the yard and slap him around. Do we?"

I'm hearing the man's got his issues. All a them do. Don't never let a necktie fool you.

"You got a boy like this?" I says. "In all due respect, now. Whatever we done it's out of love, as God is my witness. And there wasn't no slapping around this time."

"You just told me you don't know how he came by his bruises," he says.

I didn't have nothing to say to the man, then. He sure enough caught me out.

"Can you tell me exactly what the sequence of events was here, Mr. Jackson? I'm required to say I will be recording you." And the negro takes out a little tape recorder and puts it up in my face like the TV people done to Derek Jeter when he hit number three thousand. Only I'm battin' zero.

"First thing is," I says, "you ought to know I don't got nothing against negroes. That Derek Jeter's a credit to your race. Course he's half white, but you catch my drift."

This don't work—I can see it in the man's eyes. The man won't brook no smalltalk at all.

"All right then," I says, "I'll tell you plainly. The boy ran wild all night long. We didn't get five minutes' sleep. It starts out with him sitting in the corner countin' the phone book pages. Then he holds the book up like the Bible in church and slams it shut, then lays it on the carpet, then turns it sideways in this particular way, then opens it to the letter G for *God*, then closes it, then starts the whole mess all over again. All the time he's talking to himself, you can't make sense of it. After an hour Myra puts an end to it."

"What do you mean by 'puts an end to it,' Mr. Jackson?"

"Like she does. Sits him down facing the wall. Takes the book away. And so he sets to rocking and shouting, language we don't tolerate in our home, and when Myra goes to shut him up he's took his stuff out and is playing with himself, and I don't like to say this . . . but while she's standing over him he takes his shot all over her, all over his own momma!"

I didn't much feature saying that to a stranger. "You need to hear any more or does that about do you?"

"I need to hear it all," says the negro.

"All right, so then he's up and screaming, banging his head on the wall so's to injure himself, which he forthrightly does. That's them bruises you saw."

"What did you and Mrs. Jackson do when he was injured? There is no record of an emergency call."

I had to laugh at the man, I couldn't help it.

"In all due respect, sir, you got to know that *if* we had a phone out here, and *if* we rang up every time something like this happened, they'd just stop coming out to the house. And quite rightly. There's times when it's like this all day, all night long. We just manage."

"Go on," says the negro.

"So the boy's out for a spell and I tell Myra to lie down and try to get some sleep. She's been up for well on a day and a night now and with her extra weight that causes her so much knee pain. I know she's suffering. So I put her down with a pill and she's out like a light. And I finally got time for a cigarette."

It's while I'm telling the negro this that I hear the latin lady set to hollering.

"Bobby!" she's yelling. "Come back here!"

Well that boy's took off into the woods like a jackrabbit while she's filling out all her paperwork. He's *gone*, man! He can outrun me, the dogs, anyone at all with that crazy energy of his, and he's off like a shot. By the time I hear the woman holler after him he's already out of sight.

Well all hell breaks loose then. The deputies and the Child Services people forget about Myra and me and just take off after the boy, cutting through the creek in their thirty-dollar shoes and bushwhacking through the elderberry patch. I know better than to bother, because you'd never catch that boy.

Meanwhile Myra seen what happened and she sets to banging

even harder on the car window, throwing her weight around in the back seat like a unchained animal, and I can see her face is cherry red. It's the drink, I guess, and the anger, and maybe the fear of it. I'm worried for her health and I try the door, but they got it locked from both the outside *and* the inside, special police cruiser capability I guess. They got the windows mostly rolled up, and on this hot day, too, so I just shout at her through the glass to buck up, Bobby's got away. He's lost 'em. They'll tire out and give it up and everything will be right as rain.

Maybe I get through to her somehow, because all at once she goes real quiet. She's rocking a little, talking to herself, maybe praying a little Isaiah 55.

Well, the dog come out from wherever he's hiding and I decide to just let Myra be, let her calm herself while I take him for a ramble. Because what else can I do? It's not like I can spring her free of that cruiser. So Reb and me head down toward the gulch on the lookout for that coon that's been tearing up jack. I know that dog wants a piece of him and I'd truly like to give him the pleasure.

Well, it's a good long time we're out there, walking down to the spillway, checking the culverts for the coon and then heading up-gulch a bit. The wind's come up something fierce and I can see the weather's about to turn. We don't find the coon. I can hear sirens and whatnot back at the house so I just keep moving, and that's how I come to be at the Harmon place.

Rupert ain't home so I just come in through the root cellar. I go upstairs and flip on Rupert's TV and there we are. The whole thing's been blowed up into a thunderhead by the reporters. They got choppers over the woods now, I can hear 'em, police choppers looking for the boy and TV choppers looking for the police chop-pers. They got must be fifty volunteers out there combing the field, flushing every living creature out the woods—how they get that many people that fast? The dog and me must have been on the ramble longer than it felt like.

They show the creek on TV and talk about drowning, which I've gotta laugh because the boy's splashed about in that creek since before he took his first step. He never come to no harm. You can't imagine how long Bobby can hold his breath under water. We done made a game of it.

Anyway, now they got a fine-looking reporter out by the house, talking about the dog lead and holding up the boy's collar like it's a copperhead fixin' to bite her. You can't hardly make out what she's saying over the choppers. I'm just as glad of it. I don't need to hear the lies they spreading about my family.

But then the camera moves off the lady and there's the police car where Myra was, but the door's been throwed open, and there's the medics rolling my wife in a stretcher over to the ambulance, and the news lady is talking and I can't hear her, but I got to hear her now. I got to know what happened to Myra.

I'm thinking about the heat in that car and how upset the old gal was. I'm thinking, if those two cops left her in there to die, I'm coming after 'em, and the latin lady and that briggity negro from Child Services too. You're goddamn right I'm going after every one of that crew. And then they show my driver's picture on TV and a mug shot of Myra from the last time they arrested her, and our names, and it says something about Myra beat the boy and I kept him chained up like a dog, and that's it for me.

That's it.

You can understand why a man might run a little wild. I'll replace the TV, buy it on time; I told Rupert I'd make him whole. But can you blame a man for going off? All the troubles we got and they kill Myra and then put us on TV like a couple a criminals when all we did is loved that boy to death.

Well by now it's a drenching rain out and lightning too, high winds to the point where you start thinking twister. And I start thinking about my boy. He knows his way around them woods and I know he can keep out ahead of them that's chasing after him. I got no worries—I got every confidence they won't catch him.

But one thing Bobby can't brook is no thunderstorm. It's his condition. He don't like loud noises in the first place, they drive him off like wildfire, and the lightning scares him half to death.

But you know something peculiar? Myra and I never could reckon it. The boy hates the lightning, but when it gets close he runs *at* it. It's like he wants to throw down with what scares him. He's a brave kid that way, reckless. No sense of danger.

So that's what I'm thinking while the storm rolls in. The boy's going to be out there in them piney woods chasing around like the wild thing he is, giving them a run for their money, but if lightning starts to hit close he's going to hie off right out the woods toward it and they gonna to catch him. They going to haul him off and take him out his family and slap him upside the head something fierce for running off like that. I know from my personal experience. I don't want no one to set on my boy. So I shoo the dog out ahead of me and I take Rupert's hunting knife and we head back down the gulch toward that rock ridge where you can scramble down into a chokeberry patch. It's exposed for a stretch but then you're in the deep heart of the woods, along the draw where we go mushrooming. I have a hunch that's where the boy will be.

But he ain't. I can hear the choppers pretty close, maybe a half mile to the west, and I know there's going to be a lot of eyes on me any minute now. I got to think what to do. There's a rotted old cedar tree in a holler at the bottom of the draw and the dog and me dive for it. The roots are all heaved up and growed over with chokeberry, so it's a good spot to go to ground. I just need a place to lay low and think. I get myself in there and finally catch a breath.

The rain's turning into a real gullywasher, really roaring down on the treetops, but we're sheltered all right. The choppers are swinging off to the south now and it gets quieter, and that calms me down a bit. The shear's got to be hitting those chopper rotors real hard.

I'm thinking about my boy, trying to get inside his head and puzzle out where he'd go, and that picture of Myra on the stretcher won't let me be. The lightning feels like it's wanting to touch down in that swale down by the old mine spur. The storm is really coming on. I know the boy must be in a panic and I pray he ain't paying no mind to that lightning.

It's right then that the dog hears some of them hounds from a ways off and sets to baying like his life depended on it. I try to shut him up, but as usual he won't listen to nothing. I might as well be leaning on a truck horn to announce my whereabouts. And sure enough the hounds turn my way when they hear him.

I got no choice in the matter, friend. I take Rupert's hunting knife and I make it quick for the dog. He can't have felt much of nothing but he gives me one last look I'd like to forget, I'll tell you.

I got to leave him where he lay. You can't look back. That much the Army did teach me.

Now in the midst of that sad business I catch something out the corner of my eye and as I sit here and reflect I am sure it was the boy. Something green flashes by in the chokeberry and it's gone like that. It was the color of oak leaves but it was the boy's size and speed and jackrabbit way of moving. By the time I catch a good look, all I see is the woods closing up behind that green flash like nothing never happened.

Maybe the boy seen what I had to do to his dog and run off. I can't say and it don't matter now. I don't have no time to think about it. I can hear the hounds is pretty close and I figure the trackers'll follow their lead. I think to myself, *They looking for a boy but they going to find his poppa directly.*

That's when it hits me that I got to do the exact contrary of what I think the boy would do. The last thing I want to do is lead them right to him. So even though I'm thinking now that he's probably shinnied down the Bluebell Mine shaft I decide to hie back into the woods and draw them onto me. I walk right into the sound of the dogs and there's men with bullhorns hollerin' out. His name, and my name too. I keep walking, bringing it on, and I got to say I never felt calmer than in that moment, never. I don't mind saying it was a walk of righteousness.

When I step around that broke-down deer blind I walk right into them. Must be two dozen hounds and the deputy's Rottweiler, and the hounds just gather round me to mark my location, but that Rottie he come at me with a bloodlust. Fortunate thing is, I still got Rupert's knife, and I don't come out of it too bad, except for the damage the deputy does to me when he seen I killed his killer dog. He bends over and pistol-whips me in front of the whole posse—he don't care—and they got to half carry me out the woods and lay me down in the back of the squad car like a sack of feed.

And now here I sit while that latin lady, and that negro, and the whole weight of the law gets ready to come down on my old head. But there's the law of God, and the law of nature, and the law of man, and it's no secret which is the least among them. I got the consolation of the Lord and the consolation of knowing what a good thing I done for that boy.

He ain't let them find him yet, and I expect he never will. That boy has returned to nature and is part of the circle of life there. He is protected by the Holy Spirit—and if he is dead, it is the so-called Child Protective Services who are the cause of the destruction of that child, and he is with my Myra in a better place.

My prayer for the boy is that he never is found. My prayer is that when in his afflicted mind he knows the time is right, he is free to walk into the lightning and go up in a blaze of glory, if that be his wish. I got nothing against that child of God—and I know for a certainty that he can feel my love, because never did a mortal man love his son more than this man loves his Bobby.

Clemency

It is forty minutes shy of midnight by the time Hoffman finds a parking space, and the space he finds is not at all to his liking. Between the television vans bristling with satellite uplink dishes and the cars of protestors and the idling police cruisers, the streets around the Governor's Mansion are packed tight, as if it were the evening rush in a much larger town. Such a degree of confusion is unheard of at this hour—at any hour, really, in this ranch town promoted to capital by dint of being in the geographic center of the state. After circling in exasperation for twenty minutes, Hoffman takes a chance and wedges the Buick in under the crumbling Soldiers and Sailors monument, knowing it isn't a real space but hoping the police have better things to do tonight than write parking tickets. Between the protest rallies at the Governor's Mansion and the death vigil at the state penitentiary, the small force must be strained to the limit.

Crowd control's the name of the game now, Hoffman says in the privacy of his car, fingering his sparse red hair. He slips a comb from his shirt pocket and grooms his mustache in the rearview mirror, then does what he can with his flagging curls. Lately he's adopted a Colonial look, letting his curls grow out to compensate for the thinning on top, a decision that has prompted Judy, the dialysis tech, to dub him Patrick Henry. Give me ice chips or give me death, eh Patrick? she jokes as she hooks him up, but he doesn't find it funny at all.

Crowd control, he says again in the stillness of the car. And staying off television. That's what the cops are about tonight.

Hoffman locks the car and walks briskly toward the Governor's Mansion, shoulders back and eyes forward, surprised to find no one on the street. Cars and vans and pickups aplenty, but not one pedestrian or panhandler to be seen. The streetlights seem brighter than normal and he wonders if all is well at the nuclear power plant twelve miles down the river. Are the city's circuits running hot? He's often thought about the stealthy electrical pulse that leads straight back from his bedside reading lamp to the pile of decomposing atoms, and he doesn't like the implications. Lately the virulent sunsets appear to Hoffman as bruises inflicted on the skin of the sky. He prefers to close his drapes for the duration.

There is a chill on the air and he buttons his pearl-grey cardigan without breaking stride. He's a devotee of evening walks, an old-school believer in the brisk constitutional in much the same way he is a believer in late-period Mozart and chamomile tea at bedtime. He has been told that he has the predilections of a man twice his age, or perhaps a man of a prior century, either of which would be a badge of honor as far as he's concerned. So much ground was lost in the twentieth century, and the twenty-first is already a shameful mess.

It isn't that he spurns modern life. He can use a cell phone as well as the next man, but his ring tone happens to be the opening phrase of the Requiem's *Confutatis*. Such choices set a man apart. To answer to Mozart is the worthiest of rebellions.

Hoffman's wingtips ring smartly as he passes through the colonnade that leads to the statehouse plaza. When he emerges onto Washington Street he sees at a glance why the streets are so empty. It looks as though half the town is massed behind the blue barricades that have been erected, sawhorse-style, at a hundred-foot remove from the Mansion. There are klieg lights and loud-speakers, bullhorns and a fire engine, police cruisers with blue lights strobing. At the opposite end of the civic plaza, meanwhile, the ugly Capitol building sits lonely and dark, no longer spotlit thanks to state budget cuts. Hoffman stops under the amateurish statue of General Washington to take it all in.

There are two distinct groups of protestors, one easily twice the size of the other. The police have separated them with slatted snow fences of the sort one could find on any nearby ranch. The fences lend an oddly rural air to the proceedings, as if one has stumbled upon the livestock pens at the county fair. Confined, the protestors shamble in place, shifting from foot to foot, chaffing amiably with one another just as cattle might. It has been a long wait and boredom is tampering with the excitement of the event.

But as Hoffman looks on, the crowd closest to him seems to come alive. Several of the protestors jostle against the barrier and begin to chant a slogan of some kind, hiking hand-painted signs into the air as if hailing a search plane. Hoffman begins to pick his way forward carefully, hand in his pocket to guard the thirty dollars that lies hidden there, neatly tucked into an antique money clip along with three lottery tickets.

Despite the ripple of energy near the fence, the mood at the rear of the throng is relaxed. Almost at once he encounters a clump of farmers and farm wives sitting in camp chairs and passing around a six-pack of Fanta. Someone has baked a sheet cake and frosted it in pink; neatly cut squares sit atop a cooler like offerings at a Rotary Club dessert bar. It's a festive crew. One of the wives grins at Hoffman and indicates the cake with an exaggerated wave, presumably to offer him a slice. He smiles noncommittally and moves on. In a clearing a couple of town kids are smashing toy-pistol caps with rocks, setting off sharp reports that Hoffman finds unnerving and certainly inappropriate to the occasion. But then the smell of gunpowder tangs in his nostrils, a smell of childhood and summer that warms the chilly air for a moment, and he decides that he is glad the boys are there, being boys.

The deeper he penetrates the throng, the more excitement he senses around him, as if he's working his way toward some Holy of Holies. And in a sense he is. There at the front of the crowd, lit like a compact rocket by a battery of floodlights, stands a television personality whose name it will take him some minutes to recall, a trim forty-something with perfect silver hair and a red hunting vest that looks as if it was plucked from a store rack only hours before. He is interviewing a hard-looking woman who holds a sign that reads, in blood-red letters, PAY THE PRICE. She's dressed in a black teeshirt and beat-up leather jacket, her pale stomach spilling out into the cool night. The TV man leans toward her, asks a question and turns the mike her way, whereupon she snatches it from him, startling even herself. A pair of security men step forward and hover just outside camera range, flanking the famous personality in case something goes even more amiss. But when she's said her piece she hands the mike back and he quickly brings the interview to a close, scanning the crowd for another opinionmaker. The local police stand by and observe it all with detached expressions, privately entertained, perhaps, by the discomfited outsiders in their midst.

A quick scan of the protest signs around him assures Hoffman that he has chosen the right group. The slogans all advocate, with differing degrees of virulence, the immediate execution of Román Saavedra. A frail woman with cotton-candy hair holds up a crudely lettered sign carved from a cardboard box: LET JUSTICE BE DONE. Her decrepit husband's sign appeals to a higher power: LET THY WILL BE DONE. It's an older crowd, but scattered among the stooped retirees and crabbed farmers Hoffman also sees spike-haired teenagers shivering in concert teeshirts and solitary ranchers in oilskin jackets, crewcut military guys and churchy women clutching Bibles and steaming Styrofoam cups. Again Hoffman is reminded of a county fair. Were it not for the late hour and the fall chill, one could almost think it was a Saturday in August somewhere near the concession stands, the locals waiting in line for deep-fried Oreos and funnel cake and frozen lemonade. It's a crowd he knows well.

He does wonder about the bikers, though. They mill about in torn jeans and American flag doo-rags, wallets chained to their belts and eyes bright with beer or something stronger. The town does have a few bush-league bikers of its own—Riley's On First is their hangout—but there's a rough edge to tonight's crew that doesn't feel local. The capital is a way station on the long dull haul across the plains, and it's entirely possible that they're just easy riders who've invited themselves to the proceedings, not enforcers called in to make trouble. Hoffman's seen them often enough at the store, buying jerky and hemorrhoid cream, Mexican beer and generic cigarettes.

Crowd energy attracts these guys, he thinks. They see a crowd and they want in. Of course the alcohol contributes.

As if on cue, a prodigiously bearded biker in chaps walks by carrying two beer cans dangling from plastic rings. The back of his black teeshirt says

> Show Up.
> Raise Hell.
> Leave.

As he passes Hoffman, he spots an empty on the ground and sends it scudding off into the night as if kicking away a live grenade.

Beyond the snow fence, separated by a no man's land which only the media and the police seem at liberty to traverse, the opposing group's signs plead for clemency.

Don't Kill For Me! one pleads.

Death Penalty Makes Killers of Us All!! declares another.

Not in My Name! shouts a third.

Now a veteran in a wheelchair and a garrison cap pinned with medals spins forward and raises his placard: "Killer," it says simply, but the word is crossed out with a red X.

Despite the slogans, the mood across the way is placid. Everywhere candles flicker, shielded from the erratic breeze by glowing hands. Ten or twelve women have gathered into a circle and are holding hands—praying, Hoffman assumes. It is a vigil, after all. The prayers are being led, somewhat unexpectedly, by a very tall black man in a dark turtleneck and black Bobby Seale beret. A moment later the circle begins to sing a spiritual, a sort of we-shall-overcome hymn whose words are muddled by the many side conversations rippling through the plaza. As Hoffman stops beneath a roomy oak tree some of the protestors on his side of the gulf begin to chant *Jus-tice! Jus-tice!* and this moves the choristers to sing louder. But then the man in the beret ties an invisible bow in the air and brings the singing to a close. It is difficult to tell whether he is an unreconstructed Black Panther, a choir director, or both.

When the singing ends a young couple shies off from the edge of the crowd, perhaps to slip into the dark bushes and do whatever it is young couples do nowadays. Community college types, Hoffman thinks, the voice in his head tetchy. As they turn toward him he sees that they are wearing identical shirts that declare in bold green letters, "I Am Román Saavedra."

The hell you are, says Hoffman aloud. You have no idea.

No idea about what? a woman asks from close by.

Startled, Hoffman looks down to find an elderly woman sitting on a granite bench a few feet to his right. He hasn't noticed her until this moment. The woman must be in her high eighties, and she's turned out like an elegant dowager in a camel lambswool coat, a wine-red scarf and a smart fedora in forest green. Her arthritic hands, adorned with old gold, are folded calmly upon a cream cashmere blanket. Hoffman likes her at once. It isn't often that one sees someone of such obvious breeding in this town. He wonders if she's come in from somewhere else for the rally.

You said, *You have no idea,* she explains patiently. But it's not clear to whom you were speaking, or to what you were referring. I'm curious.

Just thinking out loud, says Hoffman, with a shrug that doesn't feel convincing even to him.

The owlish matron inclines her head slightly as if she hasn't quite heard him, but it's clear that she has. There is a smell of lavender and powder about her.

You're too young of a man to be talking to yourself, she says without a trace of levity. Best leave that to your elders.

After a pause she extends her elegant hand.

My name is Betsy Connor McBride, by the way.

Hoffman clasps her hand harder than he intends to, feeling the tiny bones give a little. Randall, he says. A pleasure to meet you.

The pleasure is mine, Randall.

Are you in from out of town, Ms. McBride?

Denver, she nods. When my husband died, my son convinced me to follow him out there, though neither of us prefers to speak of it in just those terms. But I was born and raised here. My daddy bred cutting horses back when you could earn a living at it.

She nods toward the clemency crowd and straightens slightly. I know a great many of those people over there and respect them very much. I grew up with some of them. In some ways I belong over there, not here.

So, what are you doing here?

She meets his eyes without hesitation.

I knew Donna Lee, Randall. I'm here to support her. To make sure that the man who murdered her goes to meet his Maker tonight.

Mm, says Hoffman, taken aback. He'd better.

You see, Randall, Donna lived next door and took care of Junie Willoughby until Junie's kids put her in a home. That was just two days before the murder. They'd told Donna she could stay on for a week until she made other arrangements. A week seemed harsh to me, because she'd been *so* good to Junie . . . officially she was just a renter, but she did a hundred little things for her. Picked up prescriptions, ordered in groceries, boiled her morning egg, that kind of thing. She's the one who called the son when Junie collapsed. She was a kind, well-mannered girl.

That's what I hear.

Donna and I would chat that summer, sitting on our porches and talking over the hedge. I had her over for meals now and then because I thought she deserved a little break from Junie. She was supposed to come for dinner the night she was murdered, Randall.

Hoffman looks away from the placid grey eyes and toys with

the buttons of his cardigan, his heart bridling. For a woman of quality she seems to want for basic tact. From the corner of his eye he can see that the widow is watching him carefully, gauging the effect of her words. There is something unnerving about her poise. He wishes she would not use his name so often.

That must have been difficult for you, Hoffman ventures.

It is difficult every day, Randall. Every day for thirteen years now, while that man's exhausted his remedies. One grows impatient for it to end.

Her voice is as neutral as if she were speaking of someone else, perhaps an Asian farmer who's lost a rice harvest to the typhoon.

So, Randall, she continues, as if there had been no talk of murder. What line of work are you in?

Hoffman looks up into the trees, relieved to be discussing something else.

I'm in retail grocery. Value Foods.

How interesting, she says, brightening. Do you own one of those stores? I remember when they opened the first Value Foods here, down near the VFW post.

Not an owner, no. It's a fortune to buy into the franchise. I'm in management.

She seems to consider this and then decides that another change in subject is warranted. After a time she says:

Not to turn your question back on you, Randall, but I'm curious what you're doing here. What's your interest in all this?

Hoffman looks away, pretending to watch the dueling television crews in the plaza. He fingers the comb in his sweater pocket, quelling the urge to take it out.

If I may ask, she adds.

I'm like anyone else, I guess. What the guy did was horrible and I want to see him pay the price.

Betsy seems to find this answer wanting. She is staring at him from below, studying him. The skin of his upper arm, around the dialysis access, has begun to itch unbearably. He's been nursing a low-grade infection around the fistula for weeks now.

Did you know Donna? she asks without preamble.

What?

Did you know Donna Lee? The victim.

Of course not. I mean, I'm sorry, but what would the odds of that be?

Not such long odds, Randall. Judging from your good manners you have far more in common with Donna than anyone else here does. It's a small place. Did you two go to school together?

I said I didn't know her.

And I heard you. But do you know what I think, Randall? I think you're not here to gawk, and you're not here to protest. Donna meant something to you and it's important to you that Saavedra die, but you're too much the gentleman to discuss it. That seems quite possible to me. You just don't look like the death penalty type, Randall.

Hoffman studies the ground before him. He should just walk away from her, but finds that he cannot.

Well, he says, maybe Saavedra's turned me into one. A death penalty type.

She seems to consider this, weighing its virtue, then says she understands. But her voice is detached now, as if something else is on her mind. She lets the awkward conversation languish, and when he steals a glance at her he sees her sharp eyes shifting back and forth as if studying a complicated equation. Hoffman folds his arms and turns his shoulders away from her to send a message, not trusting her silence one bit.

As he is studying the crowd a familiar face surges from it, stopping his breath as suddenly as the lethal injection will soon stop Saavedra's.

Not twenty feet away he sees the murdered girl pass before him at eye level. It may be only a photo pasted onto a sign, but it is as real to him as any face in the plaza. Her head is exactly life-sized, as if the crowd has parted to reveal her, youthful and very much alive, strolling toward him through the night. The airy blue eyes watch him; the delicate, expressive nose catches his scent. It is as if she is singling Randall Hoffman out from among the hundreds of protestors.

The sign carries no slogan, not even her name. It is only the face of Donna Lee, the unblemished and symmetrical face that has stayed with him these many years. He has seen it reproduced a hundred times, has studied it in newspaper articles and on television documentaries, but has never encountered it in this way, sized exactly as it was in life. At the sight of it his bad knee gives out and he nearly falls to the granite bench, coming to rest beside his elderly companion. She regards him with concern.

Are you feeling entirely well, Randall?

Hoffman's decided not to speak to her again, but in his panic the calm voice gives some comfort.

It's nothing. I'm on dialysis and sometimes it makes me feel faint.

Oh, she says, placing a steadying hand on his shoulder, I didn't realize. Are you woozy?

It'll pass.

Would a drink of water help?

Hoffman hesitates, then relents, because her solicitude seems genuine enough, and because he is very thirsty.

Betsy produces a plastic bottle from her oversized black purse and hands it to him. He cracks the seal and proceeds to drink it down in measured drafts. When he finishes she is holding her hand out to receive the empty bottle.

There's a trash can over there, he says, waving her off.

Randall, you should sit until this passes. And anyway, I'm a ruthless recycler. I'll take care of it.

She holds out her hand with a wry little smile, as if to say *I know I'm a stickler*, and so Hoffman surrenders the bottle, which she tucks carefully into her bag. Thank you, Randall. One less piece of eternal junk in the landfill.

They sit in silence for some minutes, Hoffman breathing with care, trying to clear the image of Donna Lee from his mind. He senses both Donna and the old woman watching him, which certainly doesn't help.

So, Betsy asks eventually, does the dialysis often make you feel faint?

I have to watch my fluids.

Yes, she nods. Of course. Then:

Are you sure it wasn't just seeing Donna's face on that sign that made you feel faint? So upsetting.

Hoffman brings his wingtips together and studies them carefully. He would like her to stop ambushing him in this manner. He knows her type: an old woman who thinks she can say anything to anyone by virtue of her age and otherwise elegant manners.

Looked just like her, Hoffman says.

It's hard to look at that sweet face and think what they did to her, isn't it?

They?

Saavedra and whoever his accomplice was. The other one whose semen they found. You may recall, Randall, that Saavedra had her DNA under his fingernails because she fought back, good girl, and they found his semen everywhere. But there was another man's semen, too. The police played that one close to the vest for years. They didn't want the other killer to know they had his DNA. Even the appeals judge let them suppress it. But the truth will come out, of course.

Mm-hm, says Hoffman.

Randall, is it awkward for you to hear an old woman talking so freely about semen?

Why would you say that? You're not bothering me.

Good. Anyway—I believe the police have stopped looking for the accomplice. They're holding that DNA and hoping some match will appear out of thin air.

Do you know that for a fact?

I'm certain of it.

Isn't it possible that Donna had a boyfriend? That she'd had intercourse beforehand?

I know from talking to Donna that there was no boyfriend—how she wished there were! And the location of the semen suggests that it was discharged after Donna was beaten. This wasn't a loving ejaculation, Randall.

Hm.

I've played it out in my mind so many times, Randall. Can you imagine what that's like?

——— ═══════

Before Hoffman can answer, an officious-looking woman in a navy suit approaches with an announcement.

Twenty minutes. Twenty minutes to go. This would be a good

time to up the energy, folks. Let the Governor know we're holding him accountable.

Hoffman points at the Governor's Mansion, where only a few lights are burning. Do you think he's even up there?

We know he is. We're tracking his movements. But he may be watching late-night TV, for all we know. We don't know whether his mind's made up, or if he's even listening.

Maybe he's watching us on TV. Sitting there on a nice leather couch with his feet up.

He may well be. That would be a win, I think. Anyway, he certainly knows we're out here.

And so are they, says Hoffman, nodding toward the clemency crowd.

So are they.

In your informed opinion, Betsy asks the woman, what do you think the Governor will do?

The organizer shakes her head. If it were still Governor Dell, we wouldn't be worried at all. But this new guy doesn't show his cards, does he? That's why we need to make our voices heard. So please try to rally a bit.

The three of them know that this is ridiculous, because anyone can see that neither Hoffman nor Betsy Connor McBride is the rallying type. Hoffman learned years ago to keep to himself, and it would hardly befit his companion's demeanor to chant slogans. Amid the milling farmers and frivolous kids, she presides with an elder's quiet rectitude. When the organizer moves on, she unfolds her cashmere blanket and wraps it around her shoulders. The cold is deepening as the evening ticks toward midnight. The old woman withdraws into herself again, staring straight ahead with a look of determination, as if receiving detailed military orders. They sit for a long while that way, side by side, each lost in thought.

Hoffman looks up at the Governor's Mansion just as the light in a second-floor room winks off.

Look, he says. A light just went off up there.

Then he's made his decision. He's going to bed. Shall we go?

Betsy McBride gathers her bag to her side as if preparing to leave.

You don't want to stay and find out what happens?

If it's done, it's done, and nothing you or I do here will change it. I can wait until the morning paper comes out. Can't you?

With this Hoffman's had enough of her. He begins to rise when someone in the crowd shouts *Ten minutes!* and the protesters pick it up in a rolling chant.

And then one of the television spotlights sweeps across Hoffman and the woman as if they are escapees scaling a prison wall. For a moment Hoffman is blinded.

Damn it! he shouts, shielding his eyes and sinking back to the bench. Keep that fucking light off me!

Well, says Betsy, looking at him in surprise. Just listen to you now! A different sort of man entirely.

Sorry for my language. It startled me.

We all have such strong passions where Donna's concerned.

Betsy looks away again, her gaze rising over the rival crowds, over the Governor's Mansion and Capitol building, over the giant oak that everyone says is five hundred years old. She knows her constellations, and so she knows that were it not for all the artificial light she'd be able to spot the slack-limbed W that is Cassiopeia, vain queen of the northern sky. Instead, the sky is a blank screen.

Randall, is there anything you'd like to share with me? she asks coolly, still looking up at the glowing sky.

Before Hoffman can answer, a metallic voice cuts through the night, drawing all eyes to the steps of the Capitol. While the protestors and media have been fixated on the Governor's Mansion, a podium and public address system have been quietly set in place at the far end of the civic plaza. A bank of spotlights snaps on, throwing the building into stark relief.

A man in a suit strides to the lectern and thumps at the mike to see if it's live. Caught off guard, the press scuttle toward the speaker, dodging the planters of withered chrysanthemums and the reflecting pool that has been drained for winter. The spotlights cast a gauzy haze over the nearby trees. With a great swell the rival crowds roll toward the Capitol, and in the Governor's Mansion the last light winks off.

Five minutes! shouts someone near Hoffman, but now the countdown seems irrelevant. Something is happening right now. The television cameras are transmitting live. The reporters are speaking into their mikes briskly, ready to relay whatever is said.

As the television lights turn onto the speaker, Hoffman sees that it's the Governor's spokesman, a smug talking head who's plagued the local news for weeks now. The messenger lifts his arms in a priestly gesture to quiet the crowd.

I will now make a brief statement, he says. I will not take questions afterwards.

After careful consideration of the facts and extenuating circumstances in the Román Saavedra case, and after receiving counsel from a wide range of experts and interested parties including the families of both the victim and the accused, Department of Corrections staff, and others, Governor Raines has just acted to commute the death sentence imposed on Mr. Saavedra by the Ninth District Court. The execution will not go forward. I repeat: the execution has been stopped. Further details will be given at a press conference to be held at the Governor's Mansion at noon tomorrow. Thank you for your patience and your interest in this important matter.

With this the spokesman disappears into the shadows behind the podium, hurrying off in a pack of police officers as the reporters launch questions after him. In seconds he is gone.

The rival crowds, restive for hours, are frozen in place for a long moment. It is as if a cloud freighted with winter ice has descended upon the throng, stunning it into silence.

But then a dispirited voice rises from somewhere near Hoffman. Justice, someone ventures, the rallying cry now no more than a half-hearted complaint.

Justice! comes the full-throated reply from the other side. *Justice done!* And with this the clemency crowd erupts in a jubilant roar, a pandemonium of square-dance hoots, clapping, wolf whistles. The TV crews jog toward the crowd, fast to pick the winner, cameras rolling for anyone still up and watching.

Betsy McBride leans in and touches Hoffman's arm.

It's not what you needed to hear, Randall, is it? You needed Saavedra to be silenced.

Hoffman feels a stab of pain pass like a hot wire through his head. He hasn't had a migraine in six months but tonight might break the run. The old woman goes on in her methodical way:

You know, Randall, you looked familiar to me and I realize why. You delivered groceries that summer, didn't you? Donna would order them and you'd deliver them. I remember your red hair, and the way you were trying to grow that mustache in.

Betsy Connor McBride grasps his arm with surprising strength and says:

You damn well did know Donna Lee, Randall. You lied to me.

Hoffman shakes her hand off and clambers to his feet just as one of the bikers bursts through the crowd from behind, grappling at shoulders and arms and necks until he's in the clear. He stops ten feet in front of the bench and whirls around to face the mob behind him, his black leather cap blaring the words **9/11 TRUTH** and one densely tattooed arm pointing toward the darkened Governor's Mansion.

People! he shouts. People, you just got *fucked*! Let's show that fucker up there what we think of his *bull*shit!

From somewhere on his person the biker produces a chain and swings it over his head like a medieval mace. In another setting it might be comical, but this warrior is deadly serious. Turning, he charges forward and kicks down the snow fence and tramples it under his heavy boots. A war cry rips through the night, bouncing wildly off the buildings.

Randall! pleads the old woman, rising from the bench and turning a hungry look on Hoffman. She seems oblivious to the fury around her, suddenly a little unhinged.

Talk to me, Randall. Just tell me what happened that night and I'll leave you be—

But Hoffman can barely hear her. His head is splitting and the melee is swarming around him, roiling toward chaos. Once the fence is down a hundred people fall in behind the biker and bolt across the plaza in an angry charge. The police stand by like football fans with fifty-yard-line seats. Across the way the clemency people scramble in panic and the sound of a woman's scream rends the air. The tall black man in the beret motions for calm but there is only hysteria as the wave of outrage thunders toward its target.

To steady himself Hoffman looks up at the blank screen of the sky, where to his alarm he sees Román Saavedra standing in the doorway of Junie Willoughby's house.

The killer's pocked face is a hash of red scratch marks, his bare chest sunburned and heavily ribbed. Hoffman can feel the exact weight of the cardboard grocery box in his youthful arms, can smell the boxwood hedge. He's saved the Willoughby house for last, as always, because he wants to go home with the memory of the girl leading him to the kitchen in cutoffs, her long legs and high waist electrifying, her scent a wonder as he follows close behind. He knows that on the way back to the store he will once again pull the car into a secluded cul-de-sac, unable to control himself, unable to wait until he gets back home. But this time it's not the girl who opens the door.

Hóla, Randy, Saavedra says in his smoker's voice, plucking a peach from the grocery box as if nothing is amiss. *Cómo estás?*

Randall stares at the scratched face in confusion, then takes a step backward.

Hey, amigo, relax. Come in and get a piece of that sweet little *chocho*. You know you want it, brother.

He hasn't seen Saavedra since security escorted him from the store back in May. Hoffman inherited his route when Saavedra was caught pilfering cigarettes from the delivery boxes, thinking the old people were too gone to notice. What a dumb fuck, Hoffman thought at the time: old people *live* for their cigarettes. But they didn't hire Saavedra for his smarts. They hired him because he was illegal and cheap and had his own car. They skipped the background check because background checks cost money and all he was going to do was deliver groceries, not work near the cash. No one knew he'd done time in Zacatecas and Lubbock, the one for assault and the other for armed robbery.

Saavedra tips the door open wider. Hoffman sees a box with bruised produce on the floor by the stairs and understands that this is the prop Saavedra has used to talk himself into the house. It would have been easy: she knows him as one of the two delivery men, and this is Junie's regular delivery day, though Junie is gone. Looking past the foyer, Hoffman sees a smashed lamp on the carpet and a crude smear of blood on the white wall. In the doorway that leads to the kitchen, a woman's bare leg turns slowly on the floor, as if its owner is rolling onto her back. It too is war-painted with red.

All this Hoffman sees projected in the sky above the Capitol building. And then it is gone, just as Saavedra will be gone, en route to the border, by the time Hoffman stumbles weak-kneed from the terrible kitchen with its dented refrigerator and blood-spattered drapes.

Hoffman is still staring at the sky when someone throws him to the ground. He tries to break his fall, but his knees buckle and he feels his front teeth snap sharply against the pedestal of a lamp post. His mouth fills with the taste of blood and he is aware of broken fragments loose about his gums. He spits them into his hand and shouts into the chaos around him, cursing with pain and shock and fear.

As he gets to his knees he turns to see the widow clutching her bag and searching for a path out of the chaos. Somewhere in the confusion she's lost her green fedora.

Hey! Hoffman shouts around his broken teeth. Give me back that water bottle.

Betsy Connor McBride looks away and hugs her bag closer. Hoffman gets to his feet and hurls himself in her direction, his big body a projectile speeding toward a moving target. Another biker shoves past him and then a scrawny farmer and finally a cop with his shotgun pointing toward the sky, toward the place where Saavedra's face was a moment ago. The air is bristling with shouts and screams and sirens but all Hoffman can hear is the husky voice inviting him into Donna Lee's house, and all he can see is the smear of blood glistening on the wall.

Give me the fucking water bottle! he shouts as he tackles the old woman to the ground. Her body under his is as small as the body of a child.

She rolls onto her bag like a soldier covering a grenade to save her comrades. Hoffman has some difficulty rolling her over— she is tougher than he imagined—but he manages to get a coat pocket in his grip and turn her so that she is facing him. There is no fear in her eyes. As he pins her to the pavement a gout of spit and blood escapes his mouth and falls to her cheek. Even this does not make her flinch.

Give me the fucking water bottle, he says again.

I will not, she replies, and clutches her bag as if he means to tear a child from her arms.

Hoffman tries to pry it from her grip but is stopped cold by a sharp jab to his groin. He collapses over her, stunned, and rests his forehead on the freezing pavement, praying for the spinning in his head to stop. His mind is a haze of scarlet, his mouth an open wound.

Only when he feels the old woman wriggling beneath him does he come back to his senses. Hoffman rises to a kneeling position, straddling her, and with a massive blow clouts her small head against the marble bench.

For a moment the chaos of the plaza seems to go silent. Hoffman does not know why he's hit her so hard. Her body is flaccid now, lifeless. Terrifying. As blood begins to seep through her grey hair he pries away the purse with its precious cargo and lumbers off into the dark oaks at the edge of the plaza, disappearing into the black hand of the night.

———

It is as he leans against a tree, digging in the purse for the water bottle that bears the traces of his saliva, that he realizes he is not alone.

Hey asshole, says a thin voice from the branches above.

Hoffman looks up and sees a boy laid along a fat limb like a mountain lion, the better to survey the herds pounding across the plaza. Is it one of the boys who were setting off toy-gun caps earlier? He thinks perhaps it is.

I seen what you done to that old lady. Me and my friend seen you kicking the shit out of her.

Come down here and say that.

And stealing her purse like that, too. Jesus.

Come down out of that tree.

You think I'm stupid? Besides, it won't do you no good to come after me.

Why's that?

Cause Ronnie already went to find a cop.

You little fuck, says Hoffman. Without waiting for a reply he takes off in a limping canter in the direction of his car, clutching the purse to his chest.

The Buick is exactly where he left it. He turns the key and creeps down Fourteenth Street with headlights off, checking the rearview mirror compulsively, his mouth poisoned with the metallic taste of his own blood. Ten minutes later Hoffman pulls into the Value Foods lot and parks the car around back, by the huge trash containers. He kills the engine and sits for a long while in the semi-darkness, trying to steady his breathing. A few blocks to the south, the freeway breathes roughly too, its respiration the gritty rumble of big rigs bypassing the business loop. Sirens of various kinds shear by: the woop-woop of police cars streaming into and out of the civic plaza, the mechanical klaxon of fire department ambulances out on the highway, presumably carrying the rally's injured to County Hospital. He wonders if one is ferrying an old woman to an emergency room. He wonders if she can be saved.

After several minutes Hoffman finds the courage to run his tongue over his broken teeth, then pulls a penlight from the glove compartment and in the gloom of the deserted parking lot examines himself in the rearview mirror. The damage is alarming in every way. A front tooth has been snapped in two; the right incisor has lost its tip; molars are loose in their sockets. It is as if someone has staved his mouth in with a baseball bat. At the sight of it he begins to shiver and then to sob, a sense of total loss welling up within him. He is a grown man crying in the cold shadow of gigantic trash bins.

The old woman's bag lies beside him on the seat. Hoffman clambers from the car and crosses around to open the passenger door, as if it is the woman and not the bag he is retrieving. His knee is acting up badly and as he clutches the bag to his chest and walks the short distance to the loading dock it suddenly fails him. He goes down hard on the cracked pavement littered with rotting food scraps and the oil slicks of grocery trucks. It is only the soft leather bag that spares him another injury.

Hoffman gets back to his feet and stands before the two enormous containers, each the length of a semi trailer, and tries to recall which is for recyclable boxes and which is bound for the incinerator behind the ball fields. Earlier in his career at Value Foods it was among his duties to break down boxes and corral stale-dated produce and route it all to the correct destinations, but that was when the store had its own incinerator; now, thanks to some overreaching city ordinance, everything must be shipped out. It's the stock manager who oversees it now. All Hoffman knows is that sometime in the dead of night, though he cannot say which night, a truck will come and haul off the incinerator load, leaving an empty container in its stead.

There is only one way to be certain which container is which. Slinging the purse over his shoulder, Hoffman scales the nearest one and clambers onto the lid, then inches his way on hands and knees toward the hatch. It is secured with a heavy deadbolt that would not be out of place in the engine room of a battleship. Hoffman can smell a miasma of rotting food and wonders if the huge bin is swarming with rats. It seems evident from the stench, at least, that he has chosen the correct one. He reaches for the deadbolt and finds it to be sticky, filthy with who knows what. And so, perched atop forty cubic yards of refuse, Hoffman finds himself rummaging in a dead woman's bag for something he can use to cover his hands. He finds a silk scarf; it has her lavender scent. Wrapping it around his hand, he wrenches the cold metal deadbolt out of its latch, then lifts the heavy lid with difficulty.

The container is full to the brim with refuse and Hoffman sighs with relief: the pickup must be near, perhaps this very night. He checks the purse one last time for the empty water bottle and from an excess of caution tosses the bottle as far as he can toward the back of the container, separating it from the purse and the fingerprints that no doubt cover it. Holding his breath against the stench, he reaches down into the dreck and makes a burrow for the purse beneath a mass of liquified tomatoes and bananas, then buries the bag where it will never be found. In a matter of hours, he hopes, it will be reduced to ashes, gone forever along with the bottle tainted with his DNA.

––––––––––––

Half an hour later, Hoffman stands in the hallway of his immaculate apartment and throws on the lights. It is very late—two in the morning, at least—and the heat has long since gone off. It is a point of pride with Hoffman that he sleeps with the thermostat on its lowest setting, but now he wishes the apartment were warmer. He has been shivering off and on for an hour or more now. Even the car heater could not stop it.

In the stillness of the hallway Hoffman hears a high-pitched ringing and recognizes it as the sound of his own nervous system. His nerves never rest. On the dialysis couch he's spent hours observing the peregrinations of his bodily fluids as they are gradually cleansed and sanctified. Lying awake night after night, a slave to insomnia, he has likewise studied his nervous system with scientific precision. The work of the body is relentless and obscure. Tonight, his keening nerves throw their cry against the walls, making the whole apartment ring with a shrill music he can no longer silence.

In the antique mirror at the end of the hallway Hoffman sees a liver-shaped stain on his grey cardigan and realizes that it could be his blood or it could be the old woman's. It could be, too, that their blood has been mingled in a bitter communion of life and death. By morning the sweater will be bleached to a pale cream hue and he will don rubber gloves and wring out the chlorine in the sink, the window open wide and streaming with autumn sunlight. It will be his day off; after two doses of painkillers his broken teeth will no longer trouble him. And so as the cardigan drips dry in the shower, Hoffman will brew strong coffee and consider whether it would be worth driving down to walk among the flaming maples by the river, near the levee where the sternwheelers put in a hundred and fifty years before.

THE IOWA SHORT FICTION AWARD AND JOHN SIMMONS
SHORT FICTION AWARD WINNERS, 1970–2015

Donald Anderson
Fire Road
Dianne Benedict
Shiny Objects
Marie-Helene Bertino
Safe as Houses
Will Boast
Power Ballads
David Borofka
Hints of His Mortality
Robert Boswell
Dancing in the Movies
Mark Brazaitis
The River of Lost Voices:
Stories from Guatemala
Jack Cady
The Burning and Other
Stories
Pat Carr
The Women in the Mirror
Kathryn Chetkovich
Friendly Fire
Cyrus Colter
The Beach Umbrella
Jennine Capó Crucet
How to Leave Hialeah
Jennifer S. Davis
Her Kind of Want
Janet Desaulniers
What You've Been Missing
Sharon Dilworth
The Long White
Susan M. Dodd
Old Wives' Tales
Merrill Feitell
Here Beneath Low-Flying
Planes
James Fetler
Impossible Appetites
Starkey Flythe, Jr.
Lent: The Slow Fast

Kathleen Founds
When Mystical Creatures
Attack!
Sohrab Homi Fracis
Ticket to Minto: Stories of
India and America
H. E. Francis
The Itinerary of Beggars
Abby Frucht
Fruit of the Month
Tereze Glück
May You Live in Interesting
Times
Ivy Goodman
Heart Failure
Barbara Hamby
Lester Higata's 20th Century
Edward Hamlin
Night in Erg Chebbi and Other
Stories
Ann Harleman
Happiness
Elizabeth Harris
The Ant Generator
Ryan Harty
Bring Me Your Saddest
Arizona
Charles Haverty
Excommunicados
Mary Hedin
Fly Away Home
Beth Helms
American Wives
Jim Henry
Thank You for Being
Concerned and Sensitive
Lisa Lenzo
Within the Lighted City
Kathryn Ma
All That Work and Still No
Boys

Renée Manfredi
Where Love Leaves Us
Susan Onthank Mates
The Good Doctor
John McNally
Troublemakers
Molly McNett
One Dog Happy
Tessa Mellas
Lungs Full of Noise
Kate Milliken
If I'd Known You Were Coming
Kevin Moffett
Permanent Visitors
Lee B. Montgomery
Whose World Is This?
Rod Val Moore
Igloo among Palms
Lucia Nevai
Star Game
Thisbe Nissen
Out of the Girls' Room and into the Night
Dan O'Brien
Eminent Domain
Philip F. O'Connor
Old Morals, Small Continents, Darker Times
Sondra Spatt Olsen
Traps
Elizabeth Oness
Articles of Faith
Lon Otto
A Nest of Hooks
Natalie Petesch
After the First Death There Is No Other
Marilène Phipps-Kettlewell
The Company of Heaven: Stories from Haiti
Glen Pourciau
Invite
C. E. Poverman
The Black Velvet Girl

Michael Pritchett
The Venus Tree
Nancy Reisman
House Fires
Josh Rolnick
Pulp and Paper
Elizabeth Searle
My Body to You
Enid Shomer
Imaginary Men
Chad Simpson
Tell Everyone I Said Hi
Heather A. Slomski
The Lovers Set Down Their Spoons
Marly Swick
A Hole in the Language
Barry Targan
Harry Belten and the Mendelssohn Violin Concerto
Annabel Thomas
The Phototropic Woman
Jim Tomlinson
Things Kept, Things Left Behind
Doug Trevor
The Thin Tear in the Fabric of Space
Laura Valeri
The Kind of Things Saints Do
Anthony Varallo
This Day in History
Don Waters
Desert Gothic
Lex Williford
Macauley's Thumb
Miles Wilson
Line of Fall
Russell Working
Resurrectionists
Charles Wyatt
Listening to Mozart
Don Zancanella
Western Electric